INKBLOTS

A POET'S PERCEPTION

PRAISE FOR JEFF OLIVER'S INKBLOTS

Poetry and art combine to become psychoanalysis! A fascinating experiment in combining two media to evoke even more of a response in readers than words or ink blots alone.

Reading Inkblots: A Poet's Perception made me search deep within my soul because Jeff Oliver's work gave me new insights about perceptions of both myself and my surroundings. The poetry is intensely relatable, and the original ink-blotted images created by Andrew Fremder are compelling. For poetry lovers and visually passionate people, this is must-read.

I have witnessed what true pain, suffering and horror is. Inkblots by Jeff Oliver descends into the darkest corners of the human psyche, trawling its unfathomable depths and displaying its catch in beguiling and terrifying verse!

INKBLOTS
A POET'S PERCEPTION

by JEFF OLIVER

illustrations by ANDREW FREMDER

300 SOUTH MEDIA GROUP

NEW YORK

INKBLOTS

ISBN-13: 978-1-957596-24-2

Interior Illustrations: Andrew Fremder
Foreword Taking Shape: Dave Jeffery
Cover & Interior Design: Indie Author Solutions
Published by 300 South Media Group

TABLE OF CONTENTS

FOREWORD

TAKING SHAPE

"Life is what you make it."

It's an adage I've heard countless times, said to those who are confused or in despair; a phrase brought out with intentions interchangeable with motivation or dismissal. However, life is anything but clear cut, and in moments where we need such lucidity, those times when we feel things are out of control, and the mechanisms for grasping what is going on around us are well beyond our reach, this is where our understanding of what is real and what is illusion may reflect our past experiences and their influence, perhaps defining who we truly are as individuals.

What it comes down to is a matter of interpretation. As human beings, how do we decide what is real and what is imagined? How do we define meaning in any given situation or what we witness in the moment? Maybe we merely allow things to happen and be swept away by the torrents of acceptance or ignorance. Perhaps we try to understand using the foundations of our past lived experience, to make sense of it all, and in doing so give meaning, putting our own stamp on what we see before us.

The Rorschach Inkblot Test was developed in 1921 for the purposes of determining thought disorder in severe mental illness, for example schizophrenia. The test has been developed over time so that it now encompasses predictive testing of a variety of psychological and psychiatric diagnoses, including depression and personality disorders. The essence of this test is a process whereby interpretations of images give insight into the nuances of the mind and the emotional stability of its owner, while hermeneutics - or the study of meaning - gives psychological interpretative context to those looking on. In this instance, psychiatrists and psychologists.

In contrast to Rorschach illustrative tests, Oliver has used prose to create an interpretive landscape that builds into an unfettered, surreal universe that can be determined at face value or in abstract fashion. The onslaught of brash,
stark, and often brutal imagery on show in the work takes the reader to dark places, or it can be a non-figurative place, where the chicanery of Oliver's poetry creates images of bizarre wonder and fascinating mindscapes.

Inkblots creates an interactive experience, where the reader is as much a character as those on the page. Words create images and their interpretation is for the reader to embrace and define. This is what is on show here, a stream of consciousness flowing across the pages, naked and twisted into cryptic shapes. Enhanced with Andrew Fremder's mind-bending, lavish artwork, Inkblots is, just like the illusion of life, exactly what you make it.

Now, then. are you ready to take the test?

Dave Jeffery
Worcestershire, December 2022

MISUNDERSTANDING

There's blood on my hands that's become so familiar.
I've washed them many times but the stains just won't wash clean.
I'm losing my mind as everyone talks behind me.
I can't live up to the expectations that I'm expected to be.

I'm screaming in silence and nobody hears me.
I will never be like them or learn the lyrics to their songs.
I'm fading away from what they call reality.
I will never fit into a crowd that hated me all along.

Please listen carefully.
I need you to hear.
I don't care if you love me.
I have worse things to fear.
Misunderstanding...
Is a beautiful thing.
I love when they can't do it.
I love when they cringe.
It makes me sing.
Spreading my wings.
Misunderstanding...
Is a beautiful thing.

They stand in their crowds without an identity.
Wearing many faces as they talk about each other.
I roam by myself and they keep talking behind me.
I refuse to become part of a crowd that tells my soul how to be.

I'm screaming in silence and I'm so glad they can't hear me.

I don't have to worry about which side they're on.
I'm still fading away from their crippling reality.
I will not sacrifice my peace for a crowd that hated me all along...

Please listen carefully.
I need you to hear.
I don't care if you love me.
I have worse things to fear.
Misunderstanding...
Is a beautiful thing.
I love when they can't do it.
I love when they cringe.
It makes me sing.
Spreading my wings.
Misunderstanding...
Is a beautiful thing.

TRUTH

Let me prove that madness doesn't end.

Let me show you where my reality began.
Let me talk in many shadows.
The walls are filled with screaming ghosts...

Let me introduce to you my many friends.
They will burn you into grains of sand.
There are claws in place of once moving hands.
There are prices within the hourglass...

In this place, there are no choices to be made.
Only instructions that lead to the flames.
In this place there is no way out of your shame.
You will never know what you're going to do...

What are you going to do?

Listen closely so you can understand.
Cover your ears with your now bloody hands.
This has always been the plan.
In the darkest corners of this wasteland...

The truth has always been right here.
The truth has always been your fear.
They turned into monsters when you gave in.
They turned into your darkest sin.

Your darkest sin...

In this place, there are no choices to be made.
Only instructions that lead to the flames.
In this place, there is no way out of shame.
You will never know what you're going to do...

What are you going to do?

When you refuse to become your truth.
There will be nothing left to prove.
You are a product of your abuse.
You are a product of yourself.

NEW LESSONS WITHIN

I sit here battered and bruised.
Where did my mind go?
I stay lost in my pain and torment.
I can't seem to let go.
Just a frame and a picture.
Lost memories stay unspoken and unsaid.
I can't shake these nightmares.
There are too many in my head.
I think of the stories that shake me around.
I'm beautifully screaming from the ash-covered ground.

Beast be fed!
With both bleeding fists I stand up.
I beat the shit out of my soul.
I look at my hands…
The blood just flows.
I am walking carefully around all of the voices.
They pound so loudly in my mind.
It's hard to find the truth.
There is nothing left to find.
Within a heart that is bleeding…
The past is always defined.

Each flame burns my skin.
Another boil of flesh begins.
I stay burning!
The shadows pound me with new lessons within.

My soul will be returning.
The deal has been made.
The Fire will rise.
Delivering the purpose of my pain.

I don't want to feel so comatose now.
I want to scream as I lift up the veil.
I want to be anywhere but here now.
I want to breathe to find my way out…
I don't want to feel so comatose now.

I drink down the poison.
In my hangover I wake.
I can't cry as the visions are screaming.
There is so much to take.
Horrific memories are burning within my eyes.
Is this Hell after death?
Will it ever make sense?
I crawl through the flames with nothing left.
Is this my mind?
Is this where I go to die?
This must be a dream…
I refuse to live in this lie.
The Devil calls me on the red phone down by the stairs.
I need to wake up.
Or I'm not going anywhere.
I am never alone…
The Devil sits and stares from his beautiful throne.

I don't know what to do…
I'm hitting the walls again.

I'm unsure if this will ever end.
Each flame burns my skin.
Another boil of flesh begins.
I stay burning...
The shadows pound me with new lessons within.

I'VE LOST

Inside I have died so much.
I've been waiting so long for my truth.
Inside of my mind, I have lost so much.
I am so out of tune.
Within these broken memories, there is no way back home.
I'm lost in my disbelief...
I've lost everything I've ever known.
My soul is in so much grief.

I've lost the clarity that I have always needed to be free.
I've lost my opening that I will never find down here on my knees.

I have...
Lost it.
So bad.
I'm so mad.
I have...
Lost it.
So bad.
I'm so sad.

I remember the day.
The exact hour that I lost my fucking name.
I was so afraid.
I could not fight off what I had made.
It had long sharp fangs.
It was feeding on my rage.
It opened the door to that cage.
I've never escaped it to this day.

I've lost the sanity that I left behind that day within the trees.
I've lost so many dreams and fed them to that controlling fucking
beast.

I have...
Lost it.
So bad.
I'm so mad.
I have...
Lost it.
So bad.
I'm so sad.

In time I have learned to accept the burden in myself.
I've lied so much to try to ease the burning of this Hell.
I've tried to let go of everything that holds me to the ground.
I've cried into the darkness now!

I have...
Lost it.
So bad.
I'm so mad.
I have...
Lost it.
So bad.
I'm so sad.

I still remember that day...

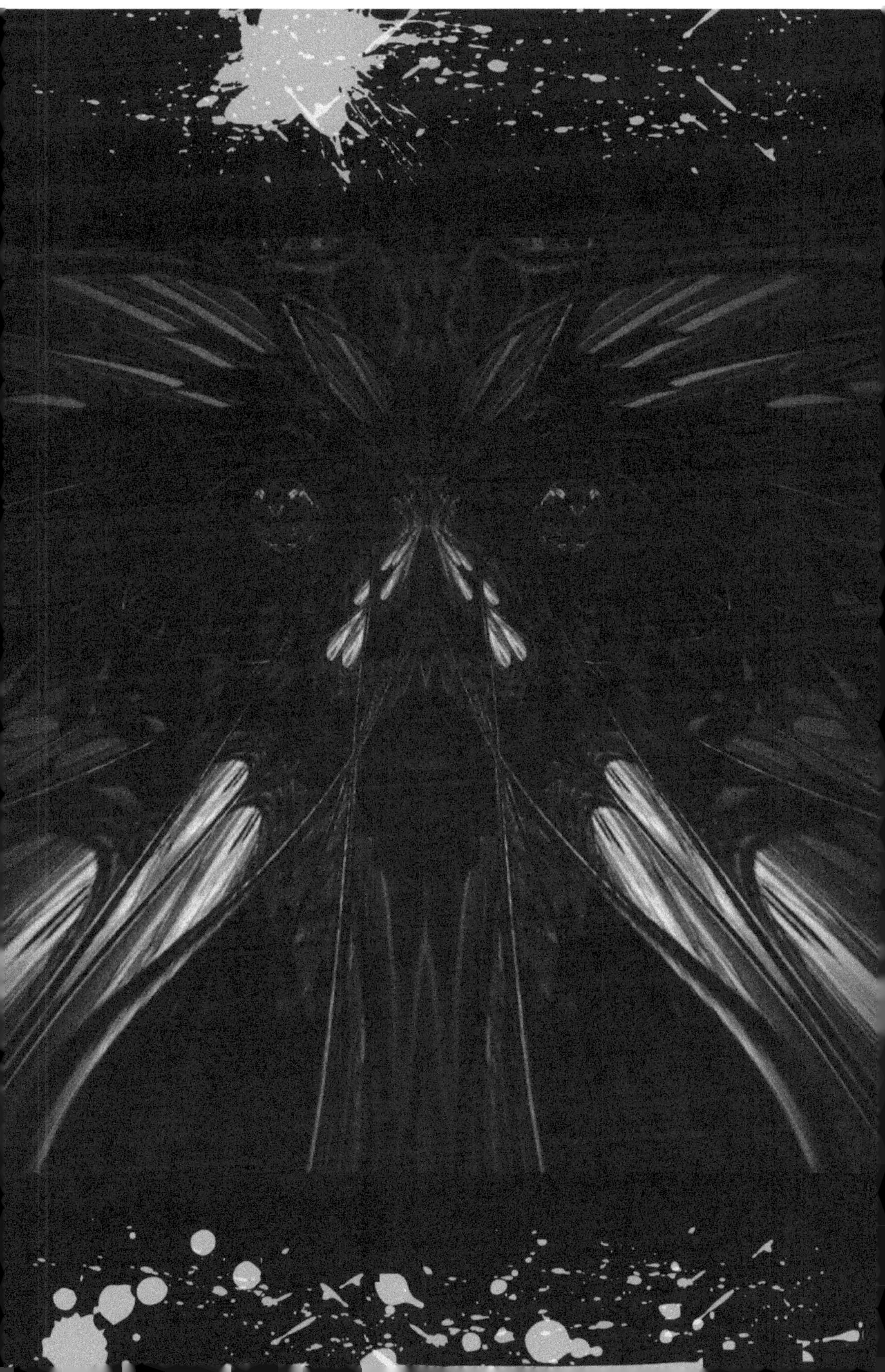

SWEET NOTHINGS

I can't remember my name.
I do not dare to try.
Remembering only introduces new nightmares.
A bloody stump where my hand used to be.
Just a bloody stump that drips and bleeds.
I'm just a lost soul trying to break free.
I'm reliving my horrible death...
I was torn apart by the trees.
Over and over I screamed.
No one listened.
I'm out for revenge now.
No soul will be forgiven.
There are many cuts covered in blood.
The world screams so loud!
The cuts!
Hell will destroy your mortal soul.
There aren't many places left to know.
I'll fuck up that mirror then rip you apart.
I'm after your soul.
I'm after your heart.
I'm creating new cuts...
I'm listening to your screams.
I love the many sounds as you bleed out!
As the toxins enter your bloodstream.
The viciousness of those towering trees is seen.
I will have you on your knees.
I am the keeper of your screams.
You called my name in the looking glass.
Your fate has now come to pass.

As I whisper sweet nothings into your ears...
The hollow shadows will extract your darkest fears.

VOICES TAKE HOLD

The voices in your head can become violent.
Telling you to do horrible things...
You must try to keep them silent.
They are controlling you with a horrific pilot.
Taking control of your mind and soul.
The wheel has been compromised.
You're no longer in control.
Your thoughts have been demonized.
They will never let you go.
Once the voices take complete control there is nowhere left for you
to go...

You must fall down into that black hole.
Then you will be falling forever.
There is no way to regain control.
You won't be able to put the pieces back together.
When the voices take hold.

The puzzle will stay incomplete...
The shadows will hide the pieces.
You must face the beast.
The beast is waiting to complete this.
Its eyes are a hollow white.
Its teeth are stained red from the many flesh filled bites.
Its claws are curved and pointing backwards.
It is not your friend and it will not do you right.
All it cares for are your screams into the night...

You must fall down into that black hole.

Then you will be falling forever.
There is no way to regain control.
You won't be able to put the pieces back together.
When the voices take hold.

The imaginary beast has charcoal colored fur that smells of rot.
It has maggots consuming the flesh that is piled at its feet.
It cares nothing about the many battles that you've won and fought.
It only cares about the tenderness of your blood filled meat.
It smells and looks like broken dreams.
It is every failure that you've ever created.
It fuels your tears as you scream.
This is the beast that you have reincarnated.
Again and again you create monsters...
One by one within your mind.
Once they are fully charged and reanimated.
They start sucking your life.

You must fall down into that black hole.
Then you will be falling forever.
There is no way to regain control.
You won't be able to put the pieces back together.
When the voices take hold.

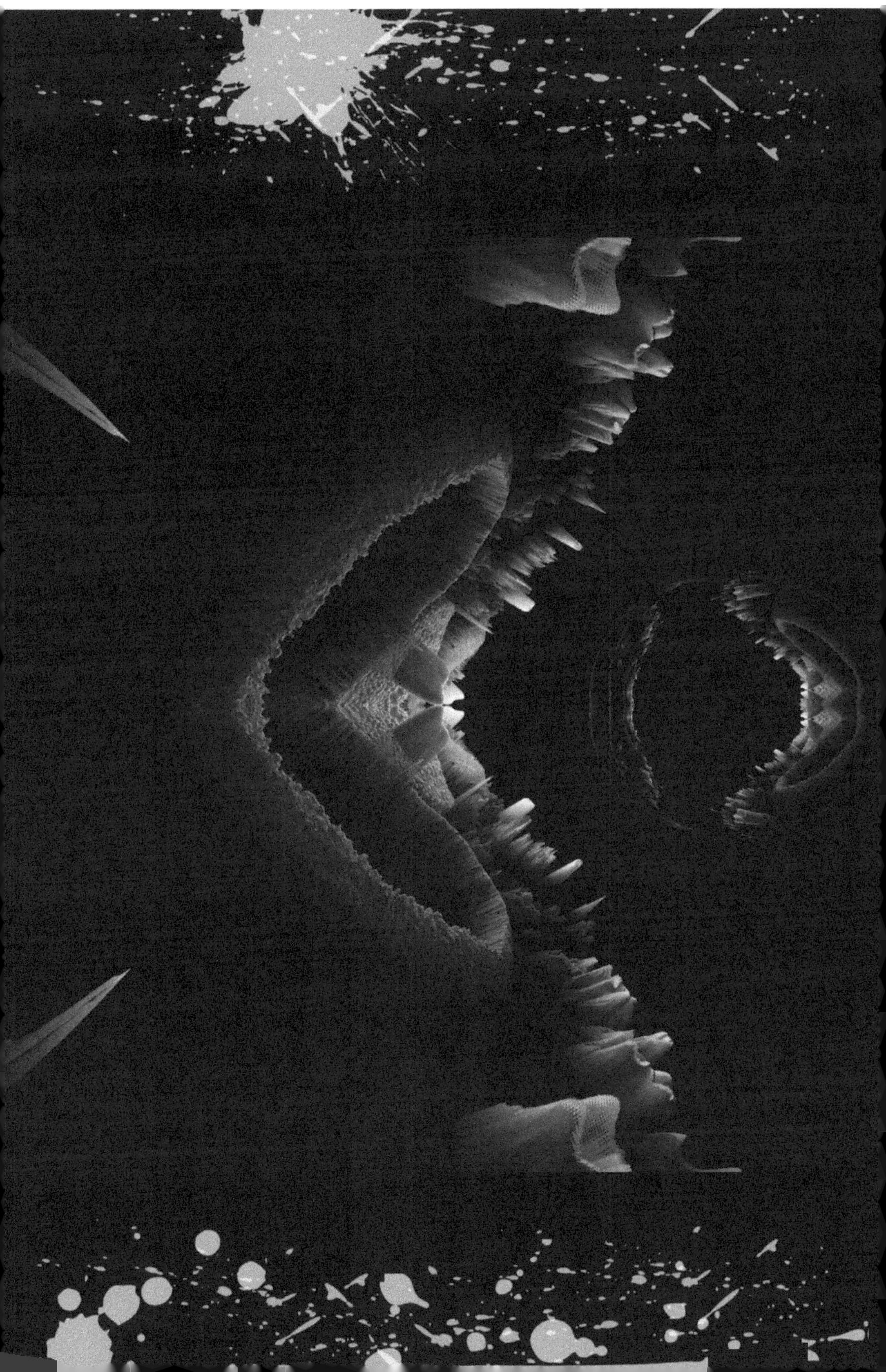

BAD HANDS

From one beautiful soul to another.
I completely understand.
I know the venom that life injects has a lasting effect.
I know what it takes just to survive and dread what comes next.
It's a cycle that lacks regrets.
Just know it's not the last time that you'll have to go through it.
It will not be your last bad hand.
When giving up seems easier.
Always remember your ambition and plans.
From one beautiful soul to another.
I completely understand...

Life will always deal us bad hands.
Life wasn't meant for us to understand.
When we can't see in front of us we can't make a plan.
Learn to embrace your bad hands.
Learn how to bluff your way through this God-Forsaken land!
We are all dealt bad hands...

I'VE EVOLVED FROM THE LURE

I'm training my mind to be a servant.
I now know that I have a greater purpose.
The negative energy that was holding me down...
Is now at my feet burning into the ground.
I've finally found myself.

The embers used to burn so deep into my eyes.
The tears would transform into emotionless cries.
The flames would burn hotter as they rose so high...
I couldn't even whisper in that place that lies.
It lied all the time.

Now that I've learned to navigate through my pain.
I can put it into words to tell myself that everything is okay.
I can let the ink speak as it blows me the fuck away.
I can stand on my feet again through the hallways of the insane.
I can finally play their games.

When I opened the door that was always locked before.
I could feel my soul leaving the places I was always supposed to ignore.
I could feel my body cooling as the fire melted that door.
I could never go back to that place that always wanted more.
I could finally move through my silence that I've always wanted to explore.

I've evolved from the lure...
Somewhat of a cure.
I guess I was never supposed to find what I was looking for.

The bloody salt water washes up on the crimson stained shore.
This place was always here while I was blind and screaming from
the floor!

I was never sure so I panicked.
I was always so weak and manic.
I couldn't hear shit through the static.
I could feel my blood seeping through the fabric.
Demons all around me pitter patter!

I'm training my mind to be a servant.
I now know that I have a greater purpose.
The negative energy that was holding me down...
Is now at my feet burning into the ground.
I've finally found myself.

I've finally found somewhat of a cure...
I've evolved from the lure.

MIXED REVIEWS

They will hate you in public.
They will love you too.
We all have to learn how to embrace mixed reviews.
They are going to keep coming at you.
From all fucking sides.
Never think of letting negativity dull your shine.
You worked hard for who you are.
You did it at all costs.
You're a shining star.
So many important things were lost.
Lost time because of passion.
Lost memories you'll never make.
Showing up late to disappointed reactions painted on each face.
Working your ass off just to become known.
Hours of bleeding, failures and fears.
Just look at how much you have grown.
You must never let mixed reviews leave you in tears.
Some of them will sting you.
Some of them will help you steer.
The steering wheel of insanity until your sorrows disappear.
Here's to all of our mixed reviews...

Cheers.

NEW MASTERPIECE

I'm falling down.
I'm falling like the leaves.
I can't cry a tear now.
I've lost the ability.
Life has beaten me down and it never seems to end…

Carry me softly through my gardens.
Carry me slowly through the trees.
This pain that I carry is forever.
Please help me from my knees.

Carry some weight that I'm holding.
Take some of this pain away from me.
I am so tired of folding.
Give me some new life to see.

I'm on the ground.
I'm screaming for relief.
I still can't cry a tear now.
Please help me find the ability.
Life has beaten me down and it never seems to end.

Carry me now through my burdens.
Carry me slowly through my dreams.
This pain of mine is forever.
Please silence my deafening screams.

Carry the scars that complete me.
Paint me a new masterpiece.

Add some new colors to my canvas.
This is not how it should be.

Life has beaten me down and it never seems to end...

Carry me softly through my gardens.
Carry me slowly through the trees.
This pain that I carry is forever.
Please help me from my knees.

Paint me a new masterpiece...

THE LIST

There are voices inside of my head that always seem to control me.
They are relentless.
I can't make sense of it.
They make me do the things that I never would have expected.
They haunt me.
They are me.

They make me lose my mind.
They are screaming all the time.

My confidence has lost its sense...
I can't be the person that the world wants me to be.

I've lost my will to live.
I have given in.

My confidence has lost its sense...
I can't be the person that the world wants me to be...

I'm lost within my sin.
The voices will always control me.
I can't fucking win.
The games are always playing.
I can't stand the list.
It's long and never ending.
The demons give me a kiss.
As my skin is fucking melting.

My struggle that I'm forced to face has always had its way.

I'm broken.
I'm still choking.
The way the world has made me lose my fucking passion.
It owns me.
It still controls me.

They make me lose my mind.
They are screaming all the time.

My confidence has lost its sense…
I can't be the person that the world wants me to be.

I've lost my will to live.
I have given in.

My confidence has lost its sense…
I can't be the person that the world wants me to be.

I'm lost within my sin.
The voices will always control me.
I can't fucking win.
The games are always playing.
I can't stand the list.
It's long and never ending.
The demons give me a kiss.
As my skin is fucking melting.

I can't stand the list!

THE CARDS

Please don't show me the cards now.
I'm not ready for that pain.
I can't stop the madness.
When it comes my way.
I get lost in the inkblots.
The shapes shift and they change.
The voices come out of the dry ink.
Then I go completely insane.
The doctors will never listen.
When I tell them to stop.
They just keep on showing me the fucking ink blots.

I told them that I would go crazy if they showed me the cards.
They refused to listen.
They would not listen.
It is breaking my heart.

They just kept on showing me the ink on the cards.
They were in for a surprise.
When I lost my mind.
When I lost my mind!

My mind is definitely twisted.
I'm harboring a nightmare within.
All I can think about is cutting into my sins.
I'm dancing in the moonlight.
It's where this all begins.
I've lost the reality here when the cards are shown again.
I just can't remember the place where I left my mind.

When I look at the ink I lose track of time.
I've told them many times not to show me the cards.
All that I can see is my reflection shining back at me from the shards.
I see blood on my hands now.
I know it's not really there.
I see blood on my face now.
The inkblots have reintroduced my nightmares.

I told them that I would go crazy if they showed me the cards.
They refused to listen.
They would not listen.
It is breaking my heart.

They just kept on showing me the ink on the cards.
They refused to stop when I lost my mind.
Sitting in this chair with my hands confined...
The cards are the reason that I've lost my mind!

There is imaginary blood now splattered on the ceilings.
In my mind I could not put up a fight.
I'm an inmate of fear.
The cards cause me to bite.
I now spin the chambers of the many imaginary guns that I hold tight.
I have many fictional knives strapped to my thighs...
I'm cutting open my memories tonight.
I cannot remember what the cards told me to do.
All that I can see is the rage that they induce.
The fake blood is dripping from the blades of my knives.
It's hard to relax through this madness.

It was designed to inflict.
I'm stabbing my haunting memories with my many blades...
I can't stop any of this!

I told them that I would go crazy if they showed me the cards.

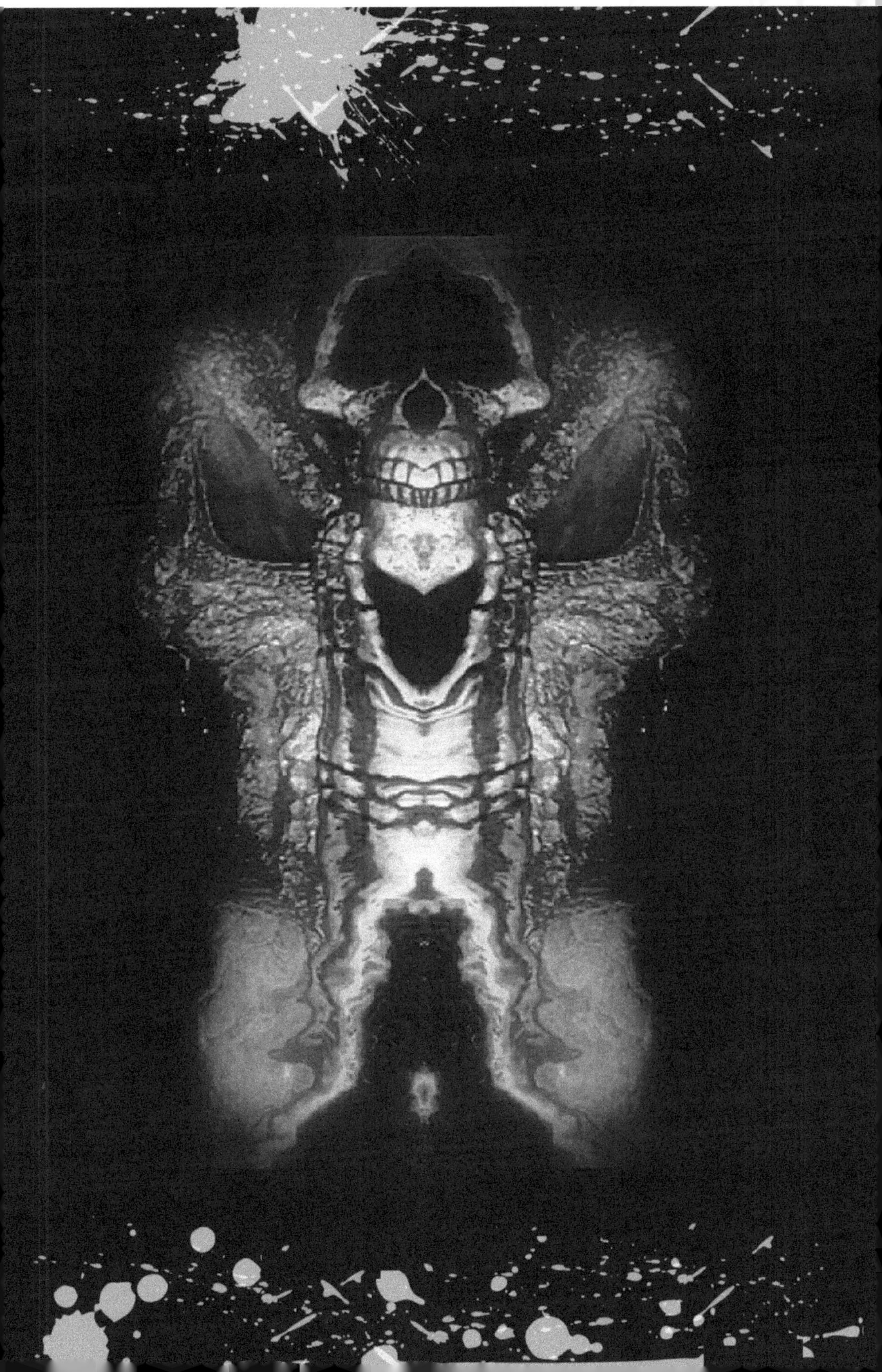

SAME

I feel so useless.
It's like I don't matter at all.
I feel so clueless.
It seems all that I can do is fall.
I'm tired of hitting these walls.
I'm tired of this all.
I just want to matter to someone.
I just want to matter.

When my heart sinks into this void of pain.
There are no flowers...
There is no rain.
There is no sunshine.
There is no light.
My vision is compromised...
I have no sight.
When my mind gets lost in this fucking maze.
There was never a fucking escape.
I've scratched and clawed for my fucking way.
Everything always ends up the same.

Everything always ends up the same...

TIMES TWO

With every mess that I make.
I've had all I can take...
Times two.

What have I become?
This pain I cannot bear.
My soul is set on fire.
It has a cold dead stare.
If I had one wish.
If I had one dream come true.
I would reach out my hands and heal all of you.

I can't see what's becoming of me.
I've always been fighting.
I've always been on my knees.
In this hold my insanity is controlling me.
It's tearing me apart.
I can't stand the pain within you.

The cold winds blow.
The cold winds blow...

With every mess that I make.
I've had all I can take...
Times two.
I can't stand your pain.
I can't stand your tears.
If I had the strength I'd make it disappear.
I would beat it down.

I would stomp it into the ground.
I would heal it all.
I would heal the sounds.

With every mess that I make.
I've had all I can take!
Times Two.

All the pain in your eyes I can see.
I'm feeling so helpless in my screams.
With you I'll bleed.
Within the divide we will be free.
Please walk into the stars with me.

I can't see what's becoming of me...

PAYING FOR PAIN

I'm opening wounds that are so familiar.
It hurts the same way each time that I bleed out.
I'm cutting away and won't sharpen my razor.
It doesn't really matter because we're all reborn again.

We are living our lives to be something we weren't supposed to be.
We are holding ourselves back from the evolution that will set us
free.
We follow the crowds out of common curiosity...
That's how they train you to become one of the sheep.

This world is crazy.
If you follow their ways.
In order to matter...
You have to sign your lives away.
Once you are programmed...
It won't matter anyway.
Once you are dumbed down.
You're on your way.
Without a say.
Paying for pain...
You know that you are...
Paying for pain!

They tell you that you're not believable and that you'll never find
your way.
They tell you to follow the orders no matter where you lay.
Then after a while you get control of your rotting brain.
You turn off the news to find a new place to play.

They tell you how to think and what you need to do.
In order to survive on a planet that lies to you.
They want full control and don't care about you.
Yet you still follow orders and every note to their songs...

This world is crazy.
If you follow their ways.
In order to matter...
You have to sign your lives away.
Once you are programmed...
It won't matter anyway.
Once you are dumbed down.
You're on your way.
Without a say.
Paying for pain...
You know that you are...
Paying for pain!

We are paying for pain!

ESCALATING EMOTIONS

We all have escalating emotions.
We write them down with pride.
Once the words hit the paper...
We know they'll never die.
Our escalating emotions will forever stay frozen in time.
One line at a time.
One scream at a time.
One dream at a time...
No wonder we are out of our minds.

We keep our minds wide open.
So our inspirations can flow.
If we are not creating...
We can't find where to go.
We are lost when we can't create brand new worlds.
We get lost in the darkness when our toes begin to curl.
Like an angry tornado our thoughts twist and twirl.
Throwing everything around us...
We get sick and we hurl.
Vomiting and piling it up disgustingly at our feet.
We clean it up then continue to hunt for the masterpiece.
The one that we can't reach.
The one that we can't see.
The illusions have clouded our thoughts permanently.
Our escalating emotions rip us apart underneath.
We are not too passionate.
We are misunderstood.
They are afraid we will pass them on the ladder.
They are shaken.

When they see the words that they failed to create.
You can clearly see the jealousy forming on their faces.
They will try their best to leave us in waste.
They are shocked when we just shake our pens and recreate.
Like magic we sporadically write their fucking masterpiece.
Like savages we rip the meat from their overflowing plates.
With class we pass them on the same mountain we've all been
climbing.
They will never be sincerely happy for us...
They never wanted us to find what we are looking for.
They want us in chains...
They do not want us to see past the binding.

We are taking the staircase...
Our escalating emotions are all over the place!

HYPOCRITICAL BABIES

Your thoughts can be deadly when you're thinking alone.
You can get forever lost in their madness with no place to go.
Flooding your mind as your head fills up.
Time just keeps on ticking as your soul explodes.
Some people think that I am an empath.
Some people think that I'm not.
I'm not a big fan of labels.
Good luck slapping one on.
I can only claim to be myself.
Just look at the fire rising around me.
Is this Hell?
Ask yourselves that before you degrade my name.
You have no chess pieces in my game.
If you're not a part of my life it's not your business what I say.
It's not your business what I do.
It's not your business how I live.
I will never come into your house questioning shit.
It's disrespectful.
It's petty.
It is simple minded and shady.
Listen up Gentleman and Ladies.
Creating labels is what drives people crazy.
Then you call us insane.
You keep throwing dirt on our names.
People are so judgmental...
People are such hypocritical babies.

If you're not a part of my life.
It's not your business what I say.

It's not your business what I do.
It's not your business how I live.
I will never come into your house questioning shit.
It's disrespectful.

If I had one wish it would be this.
I wish...
That people would mind their own fucking business.

VENOM IN THE STARLIGHT

There is an energy in our potential.
There is a pressure to succeed.
Nothing will ever drain us.
We never run out of steam.
There's an energy flowing through our spirits.
Its power is off the charts.
There is electricity gaining horsepower.
As we pour out our hearts.
There's an energy shining from the stars.
There is also venom that will tear us apart…

We will not sit in idleness.
We will not stop pursuing our dreams.
We will not let our tiredness keep us out of reach.
We are radioactive souls.
A commotion of thoughts fuse with high voltage memories.
We refuse to stay lost.
There is venom hiding in the cracks of our dreams.
It hides so professionally.
You will never see it coming until you start to scream.
There is also energy in that venom.
Be careful what you see.
Some things in the darkness can never be unseen.
It will stick and haunt your memories…

There is venom in the starlight.
There is venom within the blood that you bleed.
There is venom in every fight that brings you to your knees.
There is also an antidote hiding within the trees.

Once you find it...
Drink the entire contents of that vile.
Its contents contain the only way to battle every level of Hell.
It is the only way to battle the arachnids that feed on your rotting shell.
There is venom in the starlight...

Watch out for the Scorpion's tail.

FREE

I'm watching everything burn.
I'm full of lessons learned.
I put every emotion into verse…
I can't stand it on my own.
Please sing along.

I'm living in a curse.
I'm living in a dream.
I can hear everybody scream.
I can see the glass shattering…
Until it's gone.

I know I'll never leave this place…
So I'll make it fucking better!

In my dreams, I can be anything.
The man I've always dreamed that I could be.
I can be a Soldier.
I can be a Warrior.
I can be a Captain out at sea…

I can be anywhere at any time.
In this world that I call mine.
I can be a monster.
I can be a demon.
I can be an Angel with glowing wings.
I can be a masterpiece.
I'm a catastrophe.
I can sing so beautifully…

In my dreams I am finally fucking free.

When I write down every word.
It then comes right to life.
I can become a soaring bird.
With armor to aid my fight.
I could be a dragon breathing fire...
Watching the world burn.

When nightmares fuse with dreams.
You can hear the mixture scream.
You can see the blood red waves of the sea.
It's unlike anything you've ever seen...
And just like that it's gone.

When evil fuses with good.
The outcome is misunderstood.
The smell is like driftwood rotting away.
I embrace its beautiful decay...
As I float along.

I know I'll never leave this place...
So I'll make it fucking better!

In my dreams...
I am finally fucking free.

MEANING OF THE PAIN

It is planning out your fate.
You are burning at the stake.
You will never get away from the meaning of the pain.
When your screams begin to fade.
When your body is stuck in place.
You will never get away from the meaning of the pain.
No one hears you...
You will not be saved.
You will never get away from the meaning of the pain.

There's a fine line.
Between light and darkness.
It is hard to find.
It will make you wish that you were dead.
It enters your head.
There's a small place inside of your mind.
Where there's no time.
It makes you sick...
You can't escape here?
It's your own fears!

You've been making your mistakes.
There was always a price to pay.
You keep running right in place.
As your body continues to decay.
When the clock ceases to tick.
When the world still makes you sick.
It is too late for you to be saved...
From the meaning of the pain.

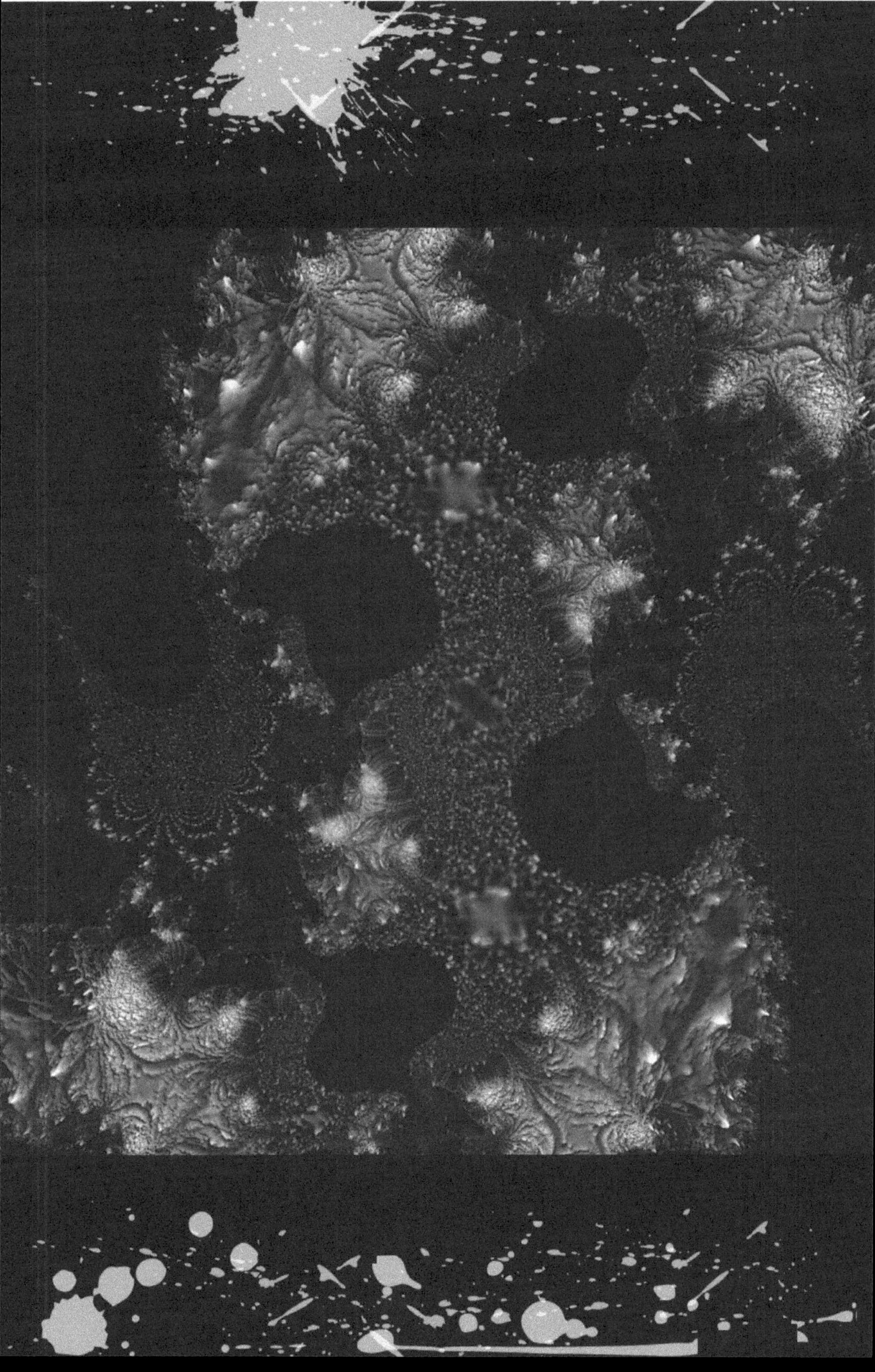

IN LOVE

There is a pleasure deep inside of me that holds my thoughts
together.
It's tempting.
It becomes me.
The thoughts control my dreams as they begin to sever.
It's haunting.
It is me.

I've lost my soul again.
This pleasure never ends.

It doesn't make sense as my eyes roll back.
Then each of my toes start to curl.

I've lost my soul again.
This pleasure never ends.

It doesn't make sense as my eyes roll back.
Then each of my toes start to curl.

I am so in love.
With every haunting nightmare.
I'm in love with the lure.
Every empty stare.
In this place of magic I don't feel so scared.
I'll be here in hell...
You can find me there.

When they rub my back and fulfill my dreams my body starts to
quiver.
I'm so numb.
I feel so dumb.
The illusions that are presented were meant to make me shiver.
I fill up.
In comes the goosebumps!

I've lost my soul again.
This pleasure never ends.

It doesn't make sense as my eyes roll back.
Then each of my toes start to curl.

I've lost my soul again.
This pleasure never ends.

It doesn't make sense as my eyes roll back.
Then each of my toes start to curl.

I am so in love.
With every haunting nightmare.
I'm in love with the lure.
Every empty stare.
In this place of magic I don't feel so scared.
I'll be here in hell...
You can find me there.

When they rub my back and fulfill my dreams my body starts to
quiver

HERE TONIGHT

My mind has crashed.
The pieces are falling from the skies.
I can't find them all now.
I have lost so much time.
My useless tears are falling.
Nobody can hear my cries.

If I could swim now...
I'd swim far out of sight.

I feel like a burden to this world.
I feel like a failure here tonight.
If I could fix everything I would change this.
I can't find my lost mind.

The rain burns like fire.
My skin is melting away from my bones.
I have lost all of my desires.
I have lost my will to fight.
The screaming voices keep on calling...
From the darkness I can't see light.

If I could swim now...
I'd swim so far out of sight.

I feel like a burden to this world.
I feel like a failure here tonight.
If I could fix everything I would change this.
I can't find my lost mind.

I'm digging my own grave.
My fingernails start to bleed.
It's hard to listen to what they say now...
There is just way too much grief.
I always feel as if I'm falling.
I still can't find relief!

If I could swim now...
I'd swim so far out of sight.

I feel like a burden to this world.
I feel like a failure here tonight.
If I could fix everything I would change this.
I can't find my lost mind.

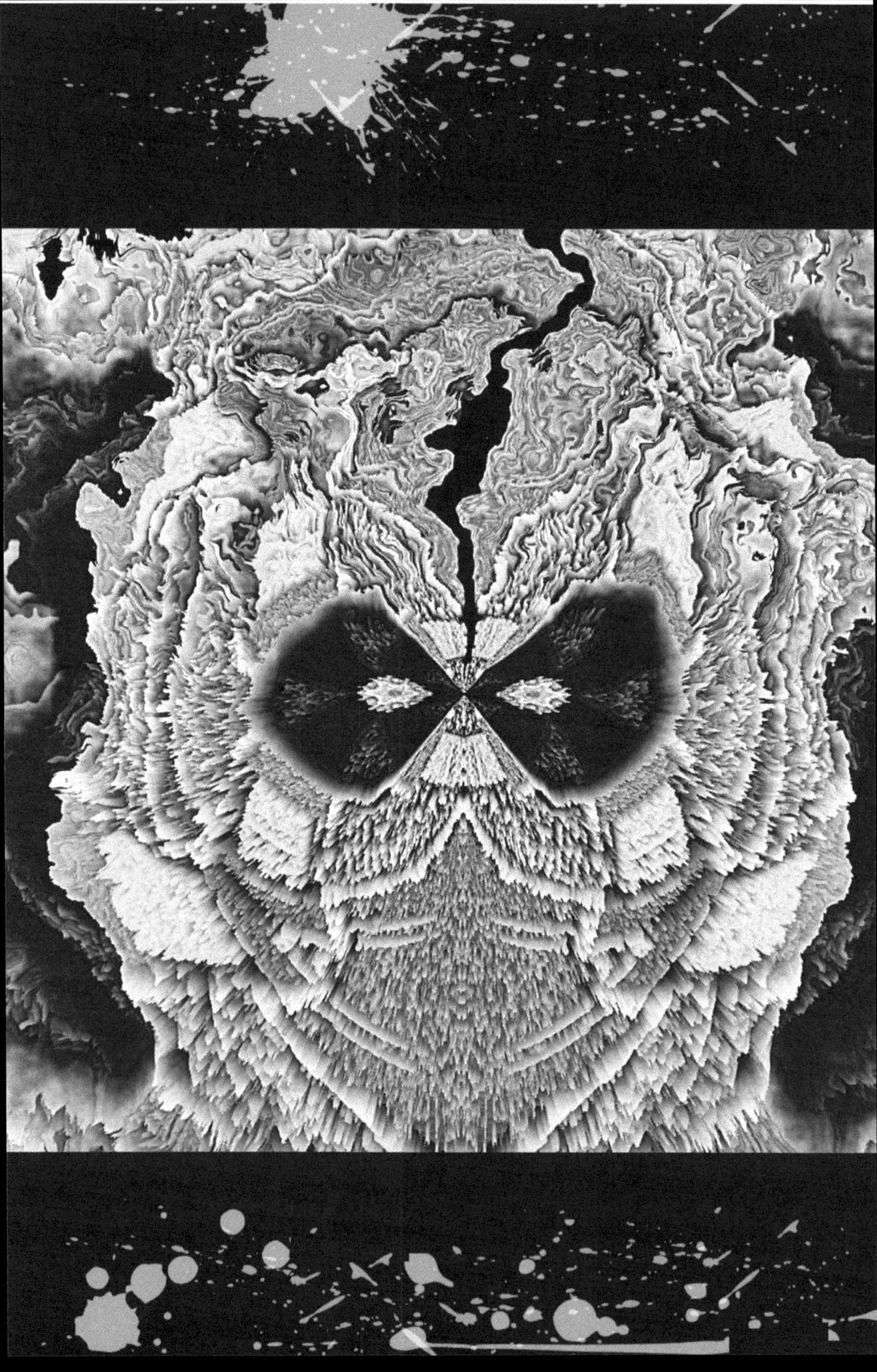

FILLING UP

Before I walk into my consciousness.
I throw up and become sick.
I throw up on all of this.
I throw up my dreams as I lose them.
Another lost ambition.
Another failure as I become sick…

My open wounds.
Are filling up.
My dreams are lost.
I've lost my will.
I've lost my will to live.
I've lost my way again and can't find peace.

I know the doors are locked.
I don't have the keys.
The way out of here is a mystery.
The flames rise up all around.
I'm screaming from the ground.
I'm throwing up again now.

My open wounds.
Are filling up.
My dreams are lost.
I've lost my will.
I've lost my will to live.
I've lost my way again and can't find peace.

I'm throwing up all over the place.

I cannot stop.
I cannot retrace.
The steps that I need to take.
There is no way back…
All ways are fake!

CHOSEN PLEASURE

I have no more words to say.
I have nothing left to fake.
This can't be undone.
This is what I have become.
I have no changes to make.
I've lost what was left at stake.
This can't be undone.
This is what I have become.

I have nothing left to blame.
All roads lead one way.
This can't be undone.
This is what I have become.
I have nothing but endless shame.
Everything that I touch I break.
This can't be undone.
This is what I have become.

Hell has broken open.
It has found my place.
I can't hide now.
And I can't run away.
It has found me here screaming into my own face.
I have chosen pleasure...
Now I must feel the pain.

I have no time to waste.
I've made too many mistakes.
This can't be undone.

This is what I have become.
I am now forced to play.
Hell's many burning games.
This can't be undone.
This is what I have become.

I have no path to fame.
I'm now forever caged.
This can't be undone.
This is what I have become.
I still don't have the words to say.
This is what I have made.
This can't be undone.
This is what I have become!

Hell has broken open.
It has found my place.
I can't hide now.
And I can't run away.
It has found me here screaming into my own face.
I have chosen pleasure...
Now I must feel the pain.

I have chosen pleasure...
Now I must feel the pain.

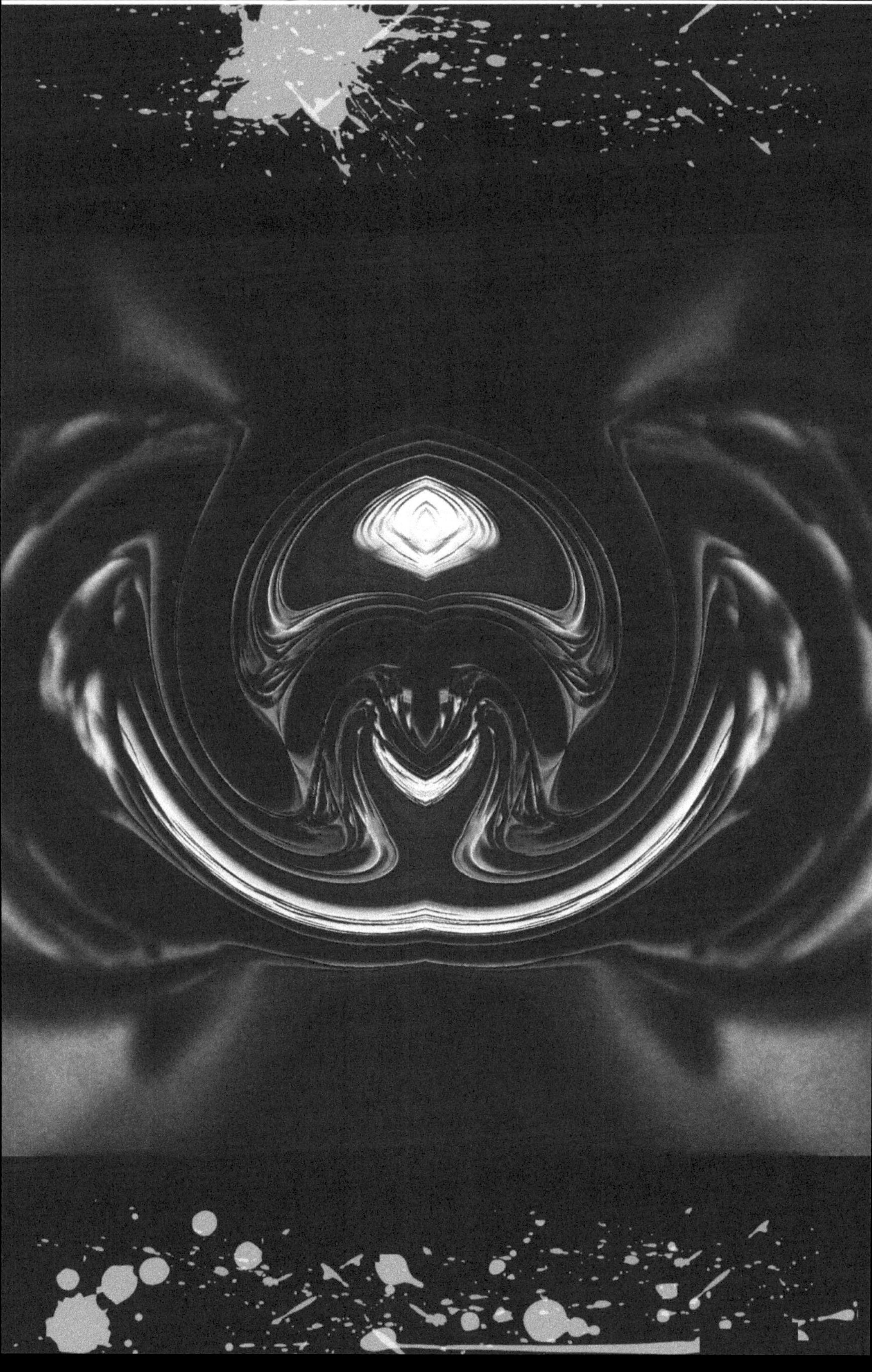

FAKE HANDS OF TIME

Darkness is a mentality that always changes course.
Darkness sings a melody with lyrics without remorse.
If you sing along long enough it will kill you at the source.
It brings so many things that will open many doors.
Open wounds are the entry way as the demons enter your pores.

Nothing ever seems fixable as you lose your fragile mind.
In madness there are fake hands of time.

Help comes when you are lost and it is always way too late.
Help comes when you've been calling it from the bottom of that
lake.
You've been singing a masterpiece about a world that you can't take.
You've been writing your tragedies and there's no way to escape.
Perfect madness laced with perfect cries as you're burning at the
stake.

Nothing ever seems fixable as you lose your fragile mind.
In madness there are fake hands of time.

The hands of time tick so fast as you waste away and lose your
dreams.
The hands are laughing so hard as you fade within your screams.
You've been writing the lyrics down and can't find out what you
need.
The shadows speak of the blasphemy as your blood flows and
excretes.
Perfect sadness laced with perfect tears as you fall down to your
knees.
Nothing ever seems fixable as you lose your fragile mind.
In madness there are fake hands of time.

BLACK AND WHITE

Within this prison of black and white.
Within our shells we scream for peace.
Nothing we ever do is feasible as nothing feels right.
Our hands reach out.
Our voices are torn away.
There are silent shouts within us as our souls decay.
Looking for the light of the day.
The colors run and still you will stay.
You're frozen in the memories of what you forgot to say...

This circle has taken you so far back.
There is nothing but fear and colors of white and black.
Your inner voice is on the attack.
You can't run from something that lurks where it always has.
You should have done this.
You should have done that.
You should have stayed longer right where you were at.
None of that matters now in your cage full of rats.
Gnawing on your extremities while you scream for the facts.
You laugh.
You react.
You cry as you're eternally attached to every fucking rodent that
bites your ass.
If you can't let them go they will always snatch...
Every fucking dream that you've ever had.
A twister gone mad.
A spiral going down and throwing the tainted sand...

The sand has covered your hands as you rub your eyes.

The ingredients are designed to keep you out of your mind.
Tasting sweet at first then switching to vile.
You're chewing on your own flesh and ingesting your own bile.
The voices will still comfort you to stay for a while.
Tricking you as the rodents feed on your denial.
The black and white spiral is only the beginning of your trials.

VIOLENT

I say hello to my reflection again.
It was never my friend.
It lies to me from the place that it lurks.
It was designed to produce pain that hurts.
In the mirror I can see the fucking truth.
The years of abuse.
Within that mirror...
It's violent.

When the glass breaks I can see my bloody face.
It's all over the place.
Within that mirror it's violent.
When the demons sing the songs that I've been dying to hear.
Things then become clear.
I then disappear.
Within that mirror...
It's violent.

When the glass shatters I can see the time I waste.
I can see the pain.
When the truth shines through it is more than I can take.
I am so insane.
Within that mirror...
It's violent.

Within that mirror...
It's violent.

BLOWN AWAY

Within this cage there's no escape.
Running in circles getting nowhere.
Eventually we will leave this place.
We will all be going somewhere.
I can't figure out the noise.
With my open wounds bleeding out everywhere.
This cage does not give me a choice.
The void does not give you time to prepare.

Listen up now.
There won't be a change.
Until the world is blown away.
This world is so foul.
This world always breaks...
You and everything right down.

No harmony.
There is no peace.
All this world will do is take.
When it explodes.
Then you will know.
The place that you were meant to be.

Fuck!

I can't breathe in this thin air.
My lungs collapse in the nuclear showers.
Nothing in this cage is fair.
The acid rain has killed the flowers.

The earth will crumble into the void.
The massive darkness will then devour.
I can't find my inner voice.
The water is now tainted with something sour.

Listen up now.
There won't be a change.
Until the world is blown away.
This world is so foul.
This world always breaks.
You and everything right down.

No harmony.
There is no peace.
All this world will do is take.
When it explodes.
Then you will know.
The place that you were meant to be.

Fuck!

ASKING WHY

I can't see through the lies...
That you tell me.
You put a spell on me.
You leave me here to cry.

I can't see through the pain...
That you give me.
You can't love me.
And I'm asking why.

You hear my screams hit the wall and echo.
You see my tears fall like rain.
You wanted to hurt me from the get-go...
You have driven me insane.
You left me screaming here in the shadows...
You left me here with my pain.

I can't see through the flames.
As they burn me.
You have cursed me.
To live in a lie.

I can't see through the hate.
As it consumes me.
As it uses me.
I'm still asking why!

You hear my screams hit the wall and echo.
You see my tears fall like rain.

You wanted to hurt me from the get-go...
You have driven me insane.
You left me screaming here in the shadows...
You left me here with my pain.

I can't see through the walls.
That I've put up.
You yell shut up!
Then my eyes grow wide.

I can't see as I fall.
So far down now.
I can't turn around now.
All I can do now is hide.

You hear my screams hit the wall and echo.
You see my tears fall like rain.
You wanted to hurt me from the get-go...
You have driven me insane.
You left me screaming here in the shadows...
You left me here with my pain.

I'm still asking why!

NEVER AN ESCAPE

Listen to the sounds of rage.
Splattered onto a piece of paper.
Burn your hands on your fucking cage.
Your blistering skin is bubbling faster.
There was never a real escape...
The illusions are made in such a pristine fashion.

There was never an escape...
You will never be okay!

What will it take?
What's going to give?
It is so hard out here to live.

Your blistering skin.
Your fire filled sins...
How do you send it all away?

You are trapped within your own mind.
You can't find the way to laughter.
As you're laughing all the time.
You can't find the things you're after.
You are confined here forever to stay.
On the walls your dreams will splatter...

There was never an escape...
You will never be okay!

What will it take?

What's going to give?
It is so hard out here to live.

Your blistering skin.
Your fire filled sins...
How do you send it all away?

You can't find the keys to leave.
You can't find the door that opens.
You can't silence the flooding screams.
Your lungs are full and you are choking.
Your mouth is sewn shut and you cannot defeat...
What the darkness keeps on provoking.

There was never an escape...
You will never be okay!

What will it take?
What's going to give?
It is so hard out here to live.

Your blistering skin.
Your fire filled sins...
How do you send it all away?

You can't send it all away!
There was never an escape...

INSTRUCTIONS

I warned the Doctor to stop showing me the cards.
The inkblots only remind me of my cutting shards...
I just don't understand why he didn't listen to me...
My instructions were not that hard.

I begged him to stop before I released this.
I begged him to stop reinventing my visions.
He screamed that he was sorry but it was too late to be forgiven.
I warned him that I would lose it.
I warned him that it would get bad.
I'm laughing mad!
He showed me the cards and I flipped out on the hand.
He was warned!
Should I feel guilty?
I didn't like him anyway...
He was greedy and filthy.
All that he had to do was listen to me.
All that he had to do was put down that deck of ink blotted cards.
My instructions were not that hard.

I'm by myself here now.
There is nobody here to keep me company.
The cards are on fire now.
I have to erase this completely.
The asylum walls now harbor flames.
I'm taking the cards down with me.
I promise you that I'm not insane...

He shouldn't have shown me the cards...
My instructions were not that hard.

IMAGINARY GUNS

There is an urge to fly deep down inside of me…
I can't shake this feeling.
It knows everything.
It brings destruction.
Within my mind that falls deep down into its own true meaning.
I scream here.
I can't see clearly at all.
I've lost so much within.
It goes so much deeper than a scream.
It is so loud that the walls fall down that I've built within me.
It goes so much deeper than a scream…

In my mind and my soul.
There is not much room to go.
Hollow eyes stare at me…
From the shadows of those trees.

Within my heart and my eyes.
There are things that just won't shine.
When darkness takes a hold of me…
My veins then begin to leak.

I have only just begun.
I'm playing with imaginary guns.

I go deeper.
I go clearer.
I wear my fears on the sleeve of my shirt.
I get meaner.

I get fiercer.
When nothing else seems to work...
I go deeper.
I scream louder.
I become quieter.
When the noise is just too much around me...
The heat burns from the fire.
I know this isn't my true reality but it feels like it to me.
I go deeper...
This is not what I call fun.
I'm spinning that barrel again in the darkness...
I'm playing with imaginary guns.

In my mind and my soul.
There is not much room to go.
Hollow eyes stare at me...
From the shadows of those trees.

In my heart and my eyes.
There are things that just won't shine.
The darkness takes a hold of me.
My veins then begin to leak...

I have only just begun.
I'm playing with imaginary guns...

I'm playing with imaginary guns. (WHISPER)

I WON'T HIDE THE GUN

There is lighter fluid on my hands.
What have I done?
What have I become?
I can't hide the gun.

There is blood all over me.
I know what I've done.
I know what I've become.
I won't hide the gun.

When the trigger went off so suddenly.
I remember that look within dying eyes.
When my sanity took over inside of me.
It could no longer be confined.

The fire that I held in my hands.
Was addictive.
Like a prescription...
That was made just for me.

I can no longer hide...
From what seemed scripted.
The darkness is predicted...
Hear me scream!

When the trigger went off so suddenly.
I remember that look within dying eyes.
When my sanity took over inside of me.
It could no longer be confined.

I won't hide the gun.
I know what I've become.
I know what I've done.
There is blood all over me...

NEVER HERE ALONE

I know I've lost my way.
Somewhere I lost my face.
In the mirror I have become...
The things that I have done.
I know I've lost my place.
That used to help the pace.
I can no longer pay.
The price has taken everything away...

The darkness consumes me.
I'm never here alone.
I can't face this...
I can't carry this load.
My arms are tired.
My body has gone numb.
I can't face the person that I have become.

I still can't find my way.
The pressure and the pain.
The mirror has become...
Every wrong that I've done.
This is the place that I hate.
It is impossible to recreate.
My happiness is fake.
The illusions are the same.
The darkness consumes me.
I'm never here alone.
I can't face this...
I can't carry this load.

My arms are tired.
My body has gone numb.
I can't face the person that I have become.

My open wounds are deep.
I'm bleeding from my knees.
Look what the mirror has done.
It has fucked my soul right up.
I know I will never escape.
There is no escape from this pain.
Everything is fake...
Please make it all go away!

The darkness consumes me.
I'm never here alone.
I can't face this...
I can't carry this load.
My arms are tired.
My body has gone numb.
I can't face the person that I have become.

I'm cursed out here on my own...
I'm never here alone!

CRAZY CAN BE BEAUTIFUL

Crazy can be beautiful in a world of confusion.
It's hard to find real balance as we scramble for fusion.
There is a fine line that separates the unstable from the stable.
We are all walking a tightrope trying not to snap the cable.
The fall will be bottomless if we slip up just once.
There are creatures emerging on the way down...
They are throwing salt into each open cut.
Crazy can be so beautiful...
Crazy can also be too much.

Crazy can fuck your life all the way up.
Crazy can also repair you when you've had too much.
Crazy can be beautiful with just the right touch.

THE BUTTERFLIES

Everything flutters here when I'm really deep in thought.
The effect of the Butterfly lays out my triumphs and costs.
I'm so lost in my own conscious mind.
My subconscious comes to the surface and eats me alive.
It opens me up like a jack o'lantern on Halloween night.

I watch the butterflies from the corner of my eye.
The colors are breathtaking.
I know they are a lie.
The colors then change to black and white.
Eliminating whatever hope that I still had alive.

The time!
Where does it go?
It sucks on my emotions as I go with the flow.
I go with what I know.
I go with what I see.
I know it's time to run for my life when the butterflies start growing
teeth.
The fluttering will then become a frenzy.
Like a salty pool filled with piranhas looking to tear some meat.
The butterflies are evil...
You must believe me!
Look at the holes throughout my skin where they've been feeding
on me.

Now can you see?
I am the madman with the beautiful butterfly wings.
I can feel fluttering throughout my entire being.

I feel the magic when the voices begin to sing.
Even though I know the butterflies were sent to destroy me...
I still love the sights...
I still love the colors that each violent butterfly brings.

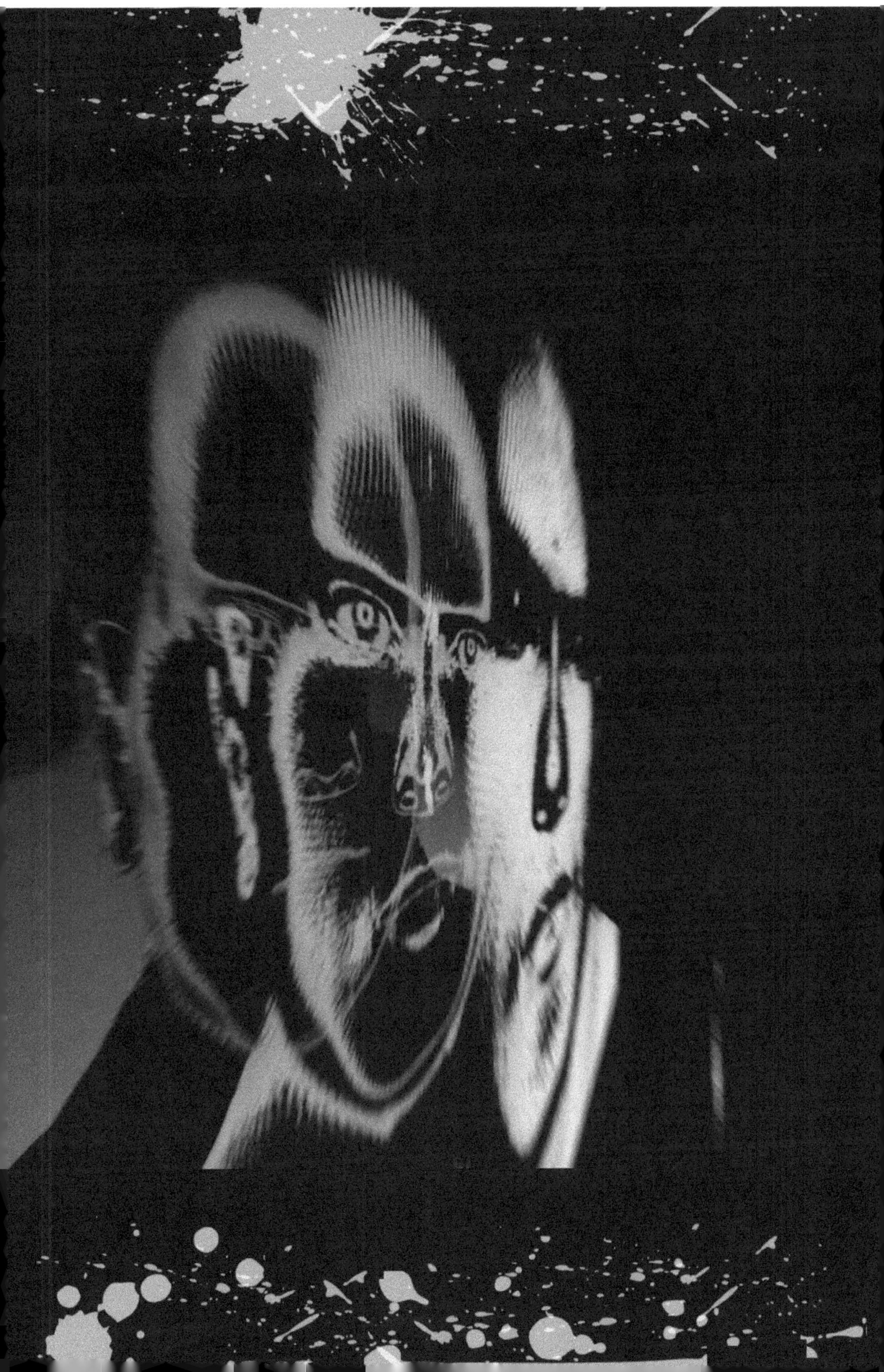

ON YOUR OWN

I've lost so much blood.
My skin begins to melt within the burning sun.
I hear the bodies thud.
I will never understand what I've become.
I am so fed up...
This is going to be so hard to overcome.

I am not ready.
I am not ready to understand.
I'm still trying to figure out what insanity is like first-hand.
Let me have a plan before you make me walk through this land.
I need a fair shot at becoming a changed man.

I've lost my way.
I've known this for years.
I repeat it again and again because this is my worst fear.
I have a price to pay.
I know That I have created this ruthless place.
This is going to be so hard to change.

In Hell there will never be guidance.
You'll see that the shadows are always smiling.
They smile because they know that there will be violence...
Hell keeps you on your own.

SORE

I'm holding my tongue again.
I'm screaming into nowhere.
I can't breathe again.
With a cold motionless stare.
Hear my cries of pain.
Echoing into shadows.
Feel my weight of hate...
There's just too much to take.

I've always been myself.
I've always searched my soul.
I've been right down to Hell.
It is so hot it's cold.
In the Devil's stranglehold.
I can't remember where I fell.

I am sore!
I am sore!
I AM SORE!

I'm bashing my head again.
Into mirrors that forsake me.
I can't see my soul again.
As the fire tries to take me.
I hear the cries insane.
I hear them in my brain now.
I feel them breathing down my neck.
Their breath just smells so foul.

I will scream so loud.
I can't hear myself.
These levels of Hell hit me so cold.
I will try to live.
I need to be free.
I need these feelings to leave.

I am sore!
I am sore!
I AM SORE!
I'm bashing my head again...
Into the mirrors that forsake me.

I AM SORE...

SNOWSTORM

I see the snowstorm reflecting in my eyes.
The sounds of nature are replaying in my mind.
I can't get the smell of pine out of my frozen nose.
Winter is here in my home away from home...

I'm running through the trees.
They've become a part of me.
Way too late to save me now...
Way too late for everything.

I'm hiding under frozen leaves.
It's too cold to rot away.
Way too late to save me now...
Way too late for everything.

I'm starting to fall asleep as my body temperature falls.
I'm starting to become numb to this all.
I can feel the bitterness of the cold winds that blow.
No one will find me as the blizzard brings the snow...

I'm running through the trees.
They've become a part of me.
Way too late to save me now...
Way too late for everything.

I'm hiding under frozen leaves.
It's too cold to rot away.
Way too late to save me now...
Way too late for everything.

I see the snowstorm reflecting in my eyes.
The sounds of nature are replaying in my mind.

LITTLE BIRD

He sees you wherever you go.
He calls you into the red rivers of sorrow.
He knows your name and knows how to twist you.
You have no idea of the horrible things that he will make you do...

First he will groom you.
He will comfort you and treat you like his own.
He will protect you.
He will guide you.
He's only buttering you up while he's heating the stew.
He's chopping up the ingredients to add to the brew.
You are the main course...
The dinner has always been you.

He has reflective eyes and stone-like skin.
He is a pasty white glistening within your sins.
He feeds on them as he continues to chew...
Holes through your midsection and all the way through you.

He never says his name.
He never says a word.
All that matters is that he is hungry...
You're in his birdcage now you little bird.
He's no longer comforting you.
He's no longer protecting you.
He's no longer guiding you.
He's preparing to consume every ounce of you.
You're now screaming in the boiling water of his stew.
Your skin starts to melt to season his brew.

You're in a birdcage now you little bird...
He's no longer comforting you.
He is watching you burn...

FLOATING

Listen to the noise.
There is no choice.
This is not the way that it should be.
I have lost my voice.
It has been torn out…
There are demons all around me…

Flames burn my skin.
I'm locked within.
This cage that harbors my every sin.
There is no help.
No relief.
This place silences every scream…

I'm floating on a sea of memories now.
A sea of dreams now.
I can't see clearly now!

I've lost my way.
In this place.
I can't find my missing face.
It's covered up.
I've had enough…
There is so much standing in my way.

Within my dreams.
Is where I bleed.
Nothing here is as it seems.
I've lost my soul.

So long ago.
The darkness has ripped it all away...

I'm floating on a sea of memories now.
A sea of dreams now.
I can't see clearly now!

I can't take the person that I have become.
That I have become.
That I have become.
I can't bear this person that I can't overcome.
That I can't overcome.
That I can't overcome...

I'm floating on a sea of memories now.
A sea of dreams now.
I can't see clearly now!

I can't take this person that I have become.
I can't bear what I should have overcome.
The darkness has spun the chambers of my imaginary guns...

I'm floating on a sea of memories now...

PITY

The void contains an addiction.
It will suck your battered soul dry.
It opens the past like a fragile hair trigger...
Exploding over and over in your eyes!

You try to wash the gunpowder out of your broken mind.
Your hands are soaked in gasoline.
You are craving the flames to rise.
You will never get your pity...

You keep on seeing the visions.
You're feeling nothing inside.
Your knuckles bleed faster while you're shattering the mirror...
There are things you just can't leave behind.

You try to wash the gunpowder out of your broken mind.
Your hands are soaked in gasoline.
You are craving the flames to rise.
You will never get your pity...

It's just another fight for you that you battle over time.
Your hands are soaked in gasoline and you crave the flames to rise.
You will never get your pity as you're losing your fucking mind.

The blood just keeps on pooling.
Pooling down at your feet.
The beast in the darkness is drooling for the flavor...
For the flavor of your tainted meat.

You try to wash the gunpowder out of your broken mind.
Your hands are soaked in gasoline.
You are craving the flames to rise.
You will never get your pity...

You're screaming within a prison.
A void that will never make sense.
You're trying to solve the puzzle of your madness in a maze that
fuels off your regrets.
You will never get your pity.

It's just another fight for you that you battle over time.
Your hands are soaked in gasoline and you crave the flames to rise.
You will never get your pity as you're losing your fucking mind.

You try to wash the gunpowder out of your broken mind.
Your hands are soaked in gasoline.
You are craving the flames to rise.
You will never get your pity...

You are out of fucking time!

IT WAS ONLY A DROP

It's hard to reach up from the gutter.
It's hard to restart your life and find another.
It's hard to breathe in a smoke filled room.
It's hard to hide in a shallow tomb.
It's hard to heal when all you do is burn.
It's hard to lift this lingering curse.
It's hard to remove the stingers from under your skin.
It's hard to stop throwing up from the venom.

It was only a drop that was injected right in.
It's all it took for the madness to begin.
It was only a drop like from the tip of your pen.
You thought nothing of it until the chaos began...
Until the chaos began.

It's hard to cover up the wounds.
It's hard to find the right words to use.
It's hard to see from inside of the womb.
It's hard each time as it is torn in two.
It's hard to be reborn again and again.
It's hard in a cycle that never seems to end.
It's hard in the place where your insanity is fed.
It's hard to find reality as it's hiding in the pretend.

It was only a drop that was injected right in.
It's all it took for the madness to begin.
It was only a drop like from the tip of your pen.
You thought nothing of it until the chaos began...
Until the chaos began.

This will not be the last time that you are born again.
The rebirth of your soul does not end.
This will not be the last time that your insanity is fed.
Your rebirth in the fire forever pounds in your head.
The flames will melt your skin residual again and again.
You will be forced to do what the voices have said.
What the voices have said.

It's hard to stop throwing up the venom.
It's hard to remove the stingers from under your skin.
It's hard to lift this lingering curse.
It's hard to heal when all you do is burn.
It's hard to hide in a shallow tomb.
It's hard to breathe in a smoke filled room.
It's hard to restart your life and start another.
It's hard to reach up from the gutter.

Until the chaos began...
You thought nothing of it until the chaos began!
It was only a drop like from the tip of your pen.
It's all it took for the madness to begin.
It was only a drop that was injected right in...

SPELL

I have always admired a bit of light in the darkness.
The kind you see as the fog rolls in.
I have always envisioned what awaits behind all of it.
Is this Heaven?
Is this Hell?
Or just a billion empty shells...
I guess I'll never be able to tell.
The beauty of the darkness has always had me under its spell.
The shadows scream.
The creatures within them reach out for me.
The sounds of delight await.
I love it here.

I must be enchanted.
How do I love it here?
It has saved me many times throughout these shattered years.
It saved me from my many demons.
Both real and make believe.
It all has its own kind of reasoning.
Its own ways to tease.
They are all around me.
Emerging from the bloody seas.
Screaming from those weeping willow trees.
Rising from the burning ground while burning down everything.
Some strike silently from the air...
In an instant they are striking.
They are all biting yet I stay.
I gave up when I learned that they will never go away.

The beauty of the darkness has always had me under its spell.
The shadows scream.
The creatures within them reach out for me.
The sounds of delight await.
I love it here.
I'm under a spell and it's clear.

OCEAN OF MY WORST FEARS

I got knocked out.
When the first wave hit.
I could not shout.
The salt made me sick.
I could not breathe.
I could not breathe!

When the storm roared.
The boat then tipped.
I can't take much more.
I can't fucking swim.
I cannot breathe.
I cannot breathe!

As the waves take over me.
I am face down in this melody.
The saltwater hides my many tears...
In this ocean of my worst fears.

I can't even scream for help.
The saltwater fills my twisted self.
The waves still hide my many tears...
In this ocean of my worst fears.

I'm full of salt sores.
The pus sacks flow.
There is no sight of shore.
As the water turns red below.
The sharks attack me...

They attack me!

I feel my flesh rip.
As each one bites.
I feel my legs twist.
No hope in sight...
Do I deserve this?
I don't deserve this!

I can't even scream for help.
The saltwater fills my twisted self.
The waves still hide my many tears...
In this ocean of my worst fears.

As the waves take over me.
I am face down in this melody.
The saltwater hides my many tears...
In this ocean of my worst fears.

The sharks have consumed me...
Now my soul is free!

In this ocean of my worst fears.

PREPPED FOR THE SHOW

Gather around for something that will make you sick.
Gather around for a surprise sharp ending twist.
Hurry up and join us, we are all right over here...
Waiting to devour you as we sense your every fear.
We love painting the walls in a crimson splatter.
A favorite color amongst the freaks.
Who you are and what you do won't matter.
As your skin starts to bleed...

We are the freaks.
We are banned.
We are in pain.
We walk with the damned...
We are the freaks.
Freaks!

Look us in the eyes as we laugh at your screams.
Tell us why you think that you should be free.
There is a reason that you've ended up here.
There is always an excuse to try to avoid the fear.
The circus is thriving and there are nothing but freaks here.
You're being prepped for the show.
The branding iron is heating up now.
Into the flames your soul now goes!

We are the freaks.
We are banned.
We are in pain.
We walk with the damned...

We are the freaks.
We are the loners!
In a world full of hypocrites with political boners.
The roles have reversed when they tried to own us.
Now they know fear.
Now they know pain.
We have nothing to lose and so much more to gain.
We offer free admission with no hidden fees.
We collect from you each time that your soul screams.

You're being prepped for the show.
The branding iron is heated up now.
Into the flames your soul now goes!

Now who's the fucking freak?
With your now abnormal looking face.
Now who's fucking weak?
With your blood all over the place.
I love the way you sob in the presence of your own broken dreams.
I love that change of pace.
I love the way that you can't stand the sounds of your own soul
crushing screams.
I love how the weight is becoming too much to take.
I've been dreaming of this price that you are now being forced to
pay.
It lights up my soul and I now lead your way.

You're being prepped for the show.
The branding iron is heating up now.
Into the flames your soul now goes!

Remember when you called me a freak?
Now I'm gonna show you exactly what that means.
I've soundproofed the walls around you.
There is no need to worry...
Nobody will hear you scream.

Now who's the freak?

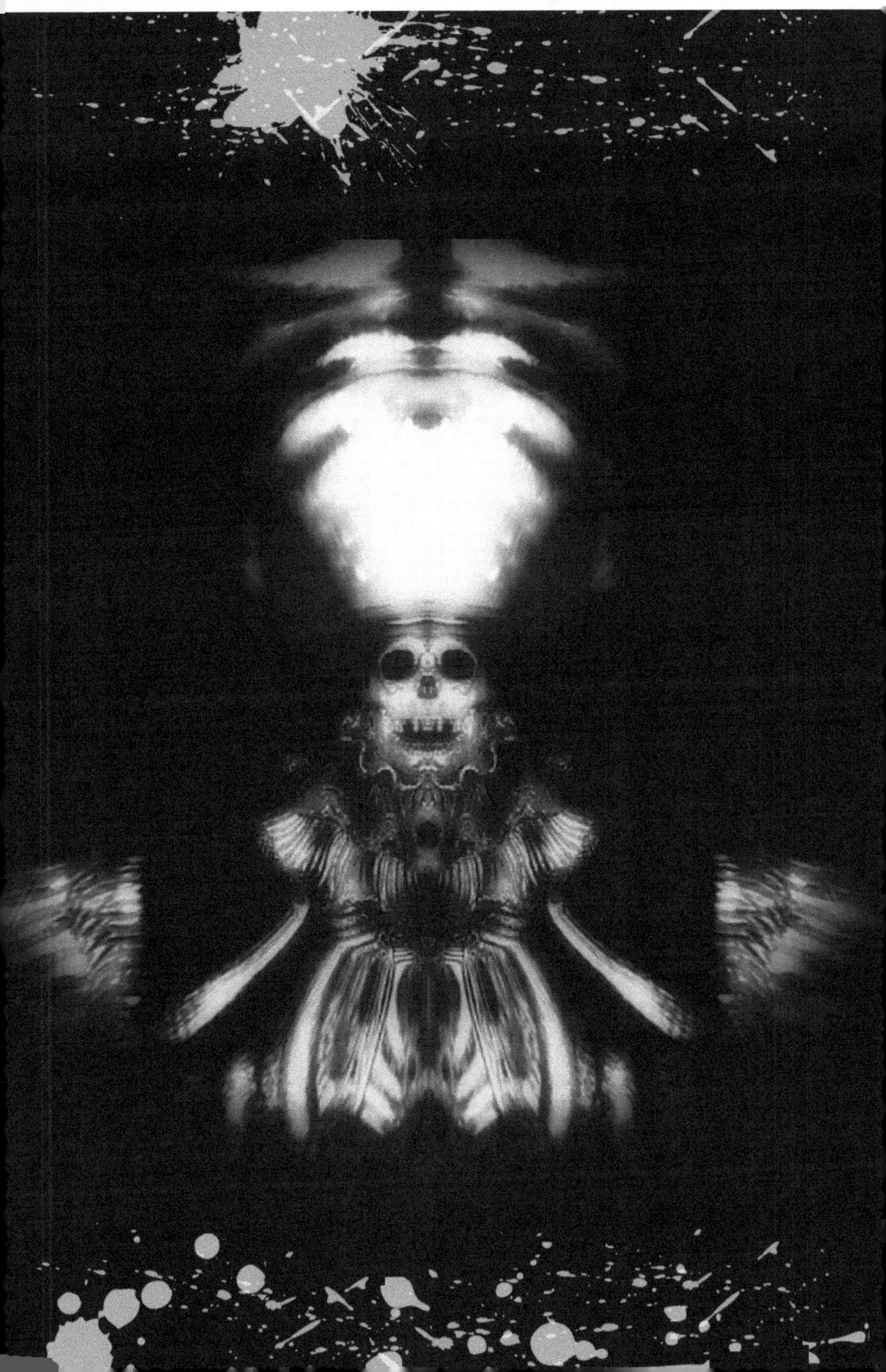

MARK OF THE BEAST

Something is burning me.
Something is not right.
Something is consuming me.
Something is lurking beyond the dimming light.
My bed is shaking.
My thoughts are fading.
My mind is blaming everything on myself.

Is this Hell?
Is this where I fell?
I'm picking up the penny that I threw into that bottomless well.
I've found my rotting shell.
I'm branded and I do not feel well.
The mark of the beast has opened my skin and the blood is leaking out.
I can't tell.
This reality is insanity in a nutshell...

I can't see in front of me.
The darkness has flooded in.
Taking all of the remaining light and sucking it from within.
Voices all around me.
Shadows trying to get in.
The mark of the beast is now branded forever into my skin.
Is that a demon or a jinn!?
I did not invite you in!
All it does is stare and laugh and I don't know where to begin...
I have now become the beast.
The mark was not intended for my sins.
It was an illusion and a passageway so the nightmare could get in.
It always wins.

HANDFULS OF BROKEN GLASS

I have handfuls of broken glass.
I'm so tired of the mirror as it laughs.
It mocks me.
It stalks me.
It knocks me on my ass.
I wonder every day how much longer that I'll last.
I can't shake the past.
I can't shake these emotions.
They overpower me so beautifully like the waves of the ocean's
mass...

I'm just a spec inside of my insanity.
I am too small for anything to matter.
Out here there is no fucking clarity.
This is the place where dreams are meant to be shattered.
Splattered.
Scattered.
Spattered onto the walls like a crime scene two doors down the hall.
Never to know who the killer was as you contemplate it all.
You continue to fall.
The void has no traces of walls.
Just an endless separation from the pain that always calls.

I still hold the handfuls of broken glass.
I still hold on tightly to the past.
I still fall on my broken ass.
I still scream into the hopeless mass.
The mass of insecurities that beat me down so bad.
The mass of my lost clarity that has driven my soul mad.

The place that laughs when I fucking fail after giving it everything
that I have.
This place is not remorseful!
It is remorseless and sad.

My bleeding hands are still holding handfuls of broken glass.

RAT

I'm talking to myself again.
I'm confused.
I can't find the line between reality and pretend.
My soul is abused.
I'm constantly lighting my fuse.
I'm mixing all of these emotions together in many open wounds.
They are excreting as they include every demon that is attached.
I'm starting to see a tail start to grow...
I'm turning into a rat.
It's a maze of madness as the flames rise so high.
It's a River of sadness...
Each way out is a lie!
The shadows again place the cheese on the trap.
My bones continue breaking...
 I hear each one of them snap!
I'm trapped as I'm fed on while my heart is still beating.
I'm being eaten alive as I'm chasing my dreams.

I am a rat.
You are a rat.
We are all rats in this fucking mouse trap.
They don't want us to evolve as we are all held down.
They hold the hammer.
They hold the nails.
Place your hands on your backs and you will feel your tails.
They only leave us crumbs of rotting cheese...
You better run fast Rat!
This planet was designed by greed.

Run Rat Run!

EVOLUTION

My time has come.
I'm reaching for the light.
My tears have disappeared now.
There is not much more to fight.

All that I know...
Is heading for the stars.
My flesh has dissolved now.
Along with my many scars.

You can't take life for granted like it's never going to end!

Follow me slowly through the forest.
Dance with me now in the trees.
Even the strong redwoods won't last forever...
That's why they leave seeds.

Follow me slowly through the starlight.
Dance with me now in the sky.
Death doesn't have to be painful...
Sing with me tonight.

You can't take life for granted like it's never going to end!

Follow me slowly through the forest.
Dance with me now in the trees.
Even the strong redwoods won't last forever...
That's why they leave seeds.

Take my dead hand within your evolution.
Watch as the time starts to fade.
Gaze at the stars that have proven...
That they all are not the same.

You can't take life for granted like it's never going to end!
Evolution is coming soon my friends...

MEANING OF THE MESS

I act emotionally more than I use logical thought.
I can't apologize for what it costs.
I'm trying to float as each leg starts to rot.
I'm opening doors whether you like me or not.
I'm flipping the coin.
I'm flipping the script.
I'm trying to silence this noise.
You know...
The sick shit.

I cannot apologize for who I am.
It just is.
Ink is leaking from my hands.
This was not planned!
You will never understand…
I'm writing for my life.
I am what kind of Man?
It's all aces.
It's all progress.
It's all healing…
I don't have time for your nonsense.
You will never understand the meaning of the mess.

You will never understand what it costs to be like this.
Let me try to explain to you my reoccurring thought process...
Everything stays the same as it changes.
Everything changes as it stays the same.
I can't escape my own personal Hell.
I still never hear that penny hit the bottom of the wishing well.

In madness dreams come true.
In madness sanity eludes you.
In order to have any trace of a clue you have to watch what you do.
One wrong step could be the fucking end of you.
One wrong move within the darkness will rip your soul right out of you.
I never asked to be this way.
I never asked to have this high of a price to pay.
It just happens and it just is.
It just progresses as I'm losing my shit.
I wish I could get rid of all of it!
I've come to terms that insanity will never make sense...
It's better for you if you never understand the meaning of the mess.

I cannot apologize for who I am.
It just is.
Ink is leaking from my hands.
This was not planned!
You will never understand...
I'm writing for my life.
I am what kind of Man?
It's all aces.
It's all progress.
It's all healing...
I don't have time for your nonsense.
You will never understand the meaning of the mess.

WHEN DESIRE WANTS TO FEED

I see a Duck.
I see a Demon.
I see a masterpiece.
I see my reasons.
I see the reasons that I am here.
I see the many things that I fear.
I feel my desires strongly in this place.
There is not much time so this is a race...

I see my open wounds all over the place.
I see my childhood's burning cage.
I see it all now...
I see my mistakes.
I see my worth.
I see my words.
I see my triumphs burning at the stake.
I see the curse.
I feel the burns...
Fire rises around me.
I feel the lure as it approaches me so silently.
Its hook contains my most irresistible need.
It's waving it around and fucking with me.
I want to grab it really badly...
I have to be stronger or it will take me.
If I touch the hook it then has me.
What is it?
I still have no idea.
It changes shapes so much to tease...

My desire is still hanging there waiting for me to snap.
I have nowhere else to go but into its grasp.
There is fire behind me.
There is desire in front of me.
There are screaming faces as far as the eye can see.
I have to embrace the desire that is presented...
I can't resist it any longer.
I really did think that I was stronger.
I'm now smothered by my desire with no air to breathe...
The legs of the demon are now crushing me.
There isn't enough oxygen left...
I can't even scream...

When desire wants to feed...
There won't be a way to break free.
My head is stuck between the legs of this demon...
They are holding me down and taking everything.

EMBEDDED

There is broken glass embedded into my feet.
There are horrible memories that I'm trying so hard to defeat.
There are beautiful demons teasing and taunting me.
Buttering me up before cutting in so deep.
The divide is gorgeous.
The divide is so magical.
It is also a lure and nothing is ever practical.
A permanent Hell turns into a permanent sabbatical.
It's laughable.
Screaming while you smile has always been so tactical.

The divide will help you find your soul.
The divide will crush your fragile throat.
The divide will snap off each one of your toes.
The divide will heal your many holes.
It all depends on which way you go.
It's a fucking coin flip...
You just never know.
The walls keep bleeding and it's making you sick.
Vomit spews from your nose.
Treat it like a raging river...
You have no choice but to go with the flow.
The divide is a mix of everything that you've ever known.
If you make a wrong turn your heart will explode.
The divide doesn't care about your fucking ego.
There are lavish gardens everywhere you go.
Let it go.
Embrace its many ghosts.
They are gifts and curses wearing the exact same clothes.

We are all on the exact same boat.
Sometimes it sinks fast.
Sometimes slow.
You never know if you will see horns or halos.
Shadows can be demons.
Demons can take away dreams.
In order to find an Angel on the divide...
First you must scream.

There is broken glass embedded into my feet.
There are horrible memories that I'm trying so hard to defeat.

PAIN BREAKS FREE

Dear Self:

I know it's my own fault for where I am.
I know I deserve to be trapped here and mad.
I just wanted people to understand.
I just wanted their blood on my hands.
I just wanted to hear them scream.
I just wanted to see what happens when pain breaks free.
It must be that monster inside of me.
It's been there all of my life.
I never unleashed it before so it was savagely hungry that night.
It requested a shattered reflection so I broke every mirror in sight.
It told me to break them and feed it the meaning of life.
The meaning of life?
I didn't understand until I looked down at my bloody wrist bands...

I didn't understand at all.
I didn't understand what it meant until I finally took that fall.
I didn't understand the blood that was stained upon my wall.
I didn't understand the voices until they were translated.
Until they were demonstrated.
Until they were created...
Right in front of my eyes I then understood what I hated.
I'm not perfect and I have many times procrastinated.
While stuck in a horrible sadness as my heart continues to stay
jaded.
My heart stays wasted while I fake this.
With all of me...
I am so relieved as the pain breaks free.

THE WASTE THAT I CREATE

In my dreams I am free.
It's the place that I want to be.
Free from hate and all of the mistakes.
As I scream there silently...

In my eyes lies a storm.
Within its eye I can't be torn.
I am free from the waste that I create.
I can't take this pain anymore...

I hold my gun behind the trees.
I'm wasting away in the rain.
I am here in screaming grief.
As the wind sings out my name...

My loaded gun is spinning fast.
I'm not sure how much longer that I will last.
The shadows talk as they laugh.
The cards run through my shattered mind.
I am damned and my time has passed.

I can't take this pain anymore...

I hold my gun behind the trees.
I'm wasting away in the rain.
I am here in screaming grief.
As the wind sings out my name...

In my eyes lies a storm.

Within its eye I can't be torn.
I'm free from the waste that I create.
I can't take this pain anymore...

HOW TO HEAL

You keep telling me how to heal from something you've never been through.
You keep directing me to do the things I don't want to do.
I love you.
I hate you.
I feel you.
I can't take you.
I can't make you understand.
I can't tell you how to plan...
For a madness that is so intense it will bury you in the burning sand.
You refuse to take my hands.
When they don't look like yours.
You will always misunderstand when I refuse to fucking land.

I fly so high.
You stay grounded.
I have opened my eyes.
You still haven't found it.
You haven't found the passageway to your soul.
You are confined to that fork in the road.
You will never be able to go...
To the places where my broken heart goes.
I love you.
I hate you.
I feel you.
I can't take you,
I can't make you understand...
I can't tell you how to plan...

For a madness that is so intense it will bury you in the burning sand.

Please don't tell me how to heal...

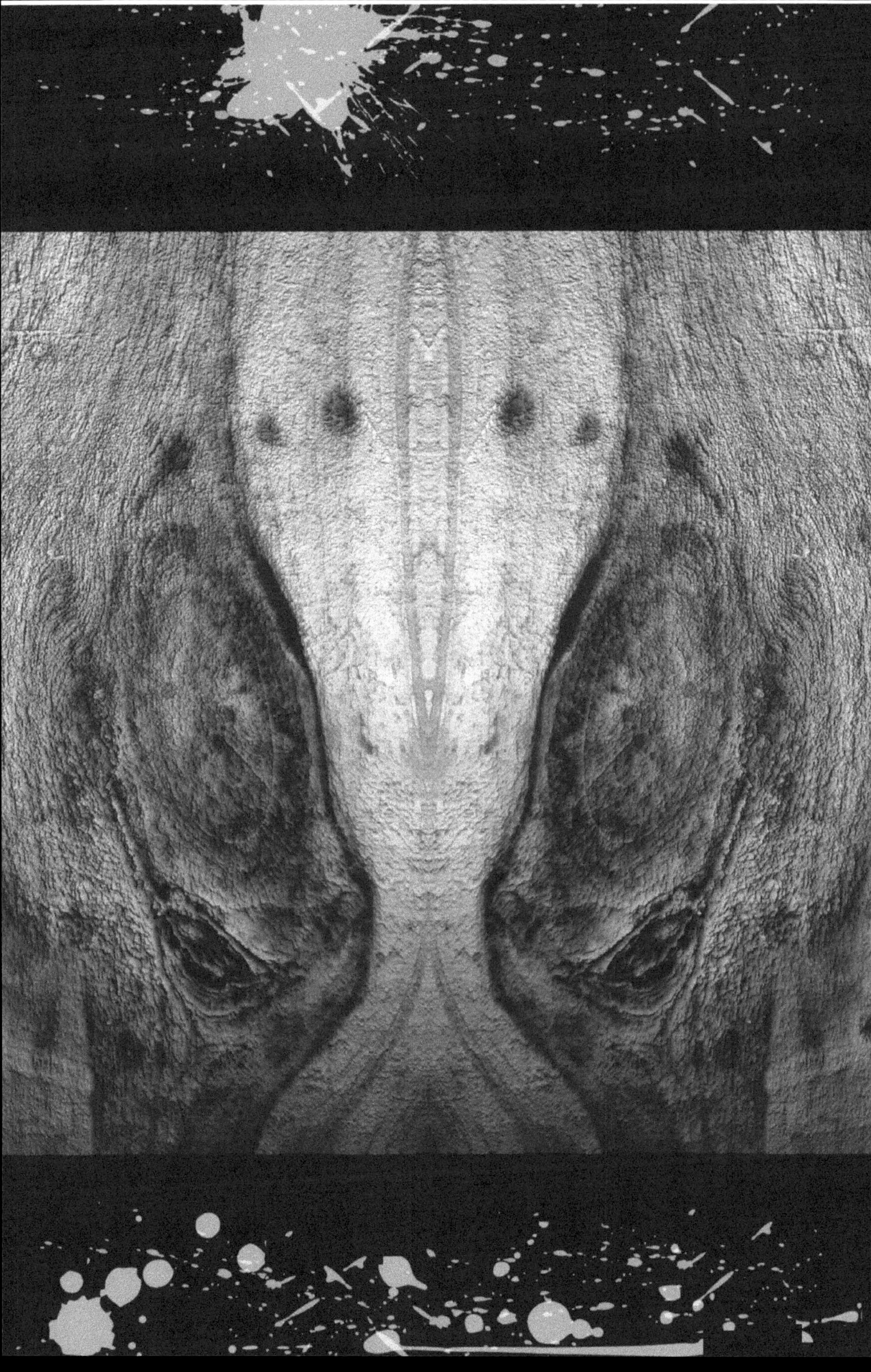

TAP

We are writing down our many dreams.
We are writing down many things.
We are losing our minds…
Or so it seems.
We are scurrying through a maze that is never ending.
Every direction feels so wrong.
Every direction that we try to go is playing the exact same song.
Walk this way the voices say.
Walk that way in this confusing place.
We are spinning in circles.
We confuse night from day.
We panicked.
We are manic.
We stay hallucinogenic.
We stay frantic!
Our confusion lies within.
The spinning makes us sick.

Running!
Running!
Running!

What the Hell is this?
What the Hell is that?
Our minds are under attack.
Where do we begin?
Confusion sets in again.
We've seen this place before.
Is this DeJa Vu?

We will never know where we are at.
We haven't a clue.
Who are they?
There is confusion within our waste.
Don't you dare think there isn't a price to pay…

Tap tap…
Tap!

On our shoulders from behind.
We turn around to look.
Nothing is to be seen within our hollow eyes.
We just want to cry.
We just want to laugh.
We just want to scream.
Is this a fucking dream?

Tap tap…
Tap!

Leave us alone!
We just want to leave this place.
We just want to go home.
The Demons just won't let us go…
Confusion lies so deep within.
The spinning makes us sick.

Running!
Running!
Running!

Demons and Monsters are sometimes Angels within dreams.
There is always so much confusion as we bleed.
These visions are consistent as they take everything.
We stay hallucinogenic in the confusion of the masterpiece.

Tap tap...
Tap!

YOU WILL NEVER UNDERSTAND

If you have never understood the darkness.
You will never understand my poetry.

You have to dig deeper than you ever have before.
You cannot be afraid of unfamiliar doors.
You can't just be certain.
You have to be sure.
Be ready for the answers that you thought you were searching for.
Darkness possesses a lure.
Once that hook goes in it will always crave more.
The bait is the deterrent.
The bait is what you see.
Little did you know it had a barbed hook underneath.
Did you bite it out of hunger?
Did you bite it just to see?
Don't clamp down on it unless you are sure you are ready.
Darkness is not a game.
Darkness is not a claim to fame.
Darkness fuels the illusions of the comfort that it creates.
Darkness gives way less than it takes.
The shadows do not give a shit about what it takes.
They just take it.
They just leave you wasted.
It was the plan all along as your soul faded.
Some say that darkness is their friend.
Some say it's the way that they fit in.
That's when you become full of shit…
Darkness is never going to let you win.

It just takes everything out of you while fucking you over in your
own sins.

If you have never understood the darkness.
You will never understand my poetry.

TELL ME HOW

Listen to the sounds of hate.
Taking over everything around you.
The people here have gone insane.
They have learned to perfect the abuse.
Nothing ever stays the same...
Open minds are caged forever.
Everything continues to change.
In a world that demonstrates.
That it will never stop the pain.
We are lost and so deranged...

Please tell me how.
Please tell me when...
I can escape these rising flames.
I need a hand.
I need a way...
To find myself again.
I need some help.
I need some love.
Please take this all away...

A one way path that leads to the edge.
One foot out and I'm getting closer.
Tell me how to smile again.
I'm so lost and almost completely over.
What is left to fucking defend?
I have lost my four leaf clover.
I can't stop the voices in my head.
They are in control and becoming colder.

When will this fucking madness end?
The demons are sitting on my shoulders...

Please tell me how.
Please tell me when...
I can escape these rising flames.
I need a hand.
I need a way...
To find myself again.
I need some help.
I need some love.
Please take this all away...

Please tell me how!

FEVER LAND

I'm walking through a place that I can't bear.
The looking glass is laughing as I give it a glare.
It hates me.
I know that it does.
It only reminds me of who I've become.
My soul has to run.
I'm a loaded fucking gun.
When my emotions conspire I keep hearing that voice that says:
"You Fuckup".
Suck it up buttercup...
It's not that bad.
While blood is leaking from my head as I'm screaming mad.
The darkness has a plan.
It takes me away to FEVER LAND.
That's what I call it.
The other names are taken.
There's sweat running down my cheeks and I'm fucking shaking...

This explanation will take a bit longer.
I hope you have a good stomach...
If not it needs to get stronger.
When a demon begins to tear into your flesh.
It begins softly before the final mess.
It has to first get into your head.
Learning every flaw and your hidden regrets.
Learning every desire that you've ever had.
As it's fucking you beautifully in FEVER LAND.
Caressing and kissing.
Understanding and glistening.

Warm-hearted as it's listening...
To your tortured soul.
It's digging a hole deep within your mind.
The one that you've spent years trying to find.
Your darkness is one of a kind.
It's intoxicating juices then turn sickening.
Smelling of rot as you see the pus sacks blistering.
It became a surprise when the tables were turned.
It became a nightmare when it started to burn.
Visions of worms.
Visions of imprisonment.
Visions of a curse...
A curse placed on your given name!

Visions of white walls while you're bouncing off of them deranged.
Millions of screaming, reaching hands.
With a sign that says "WELCOME TO FEVER LAND".
A place that you will never fully understand.
When you finally think that you've got it all figured out...
The walls change colors and floor plans.
Then you have to start screaming all over again...
A residual pace awaits behind the mirror that was busted by your hands...
That pace will kill you...
That place is FEVER LAND.

Do you understand?

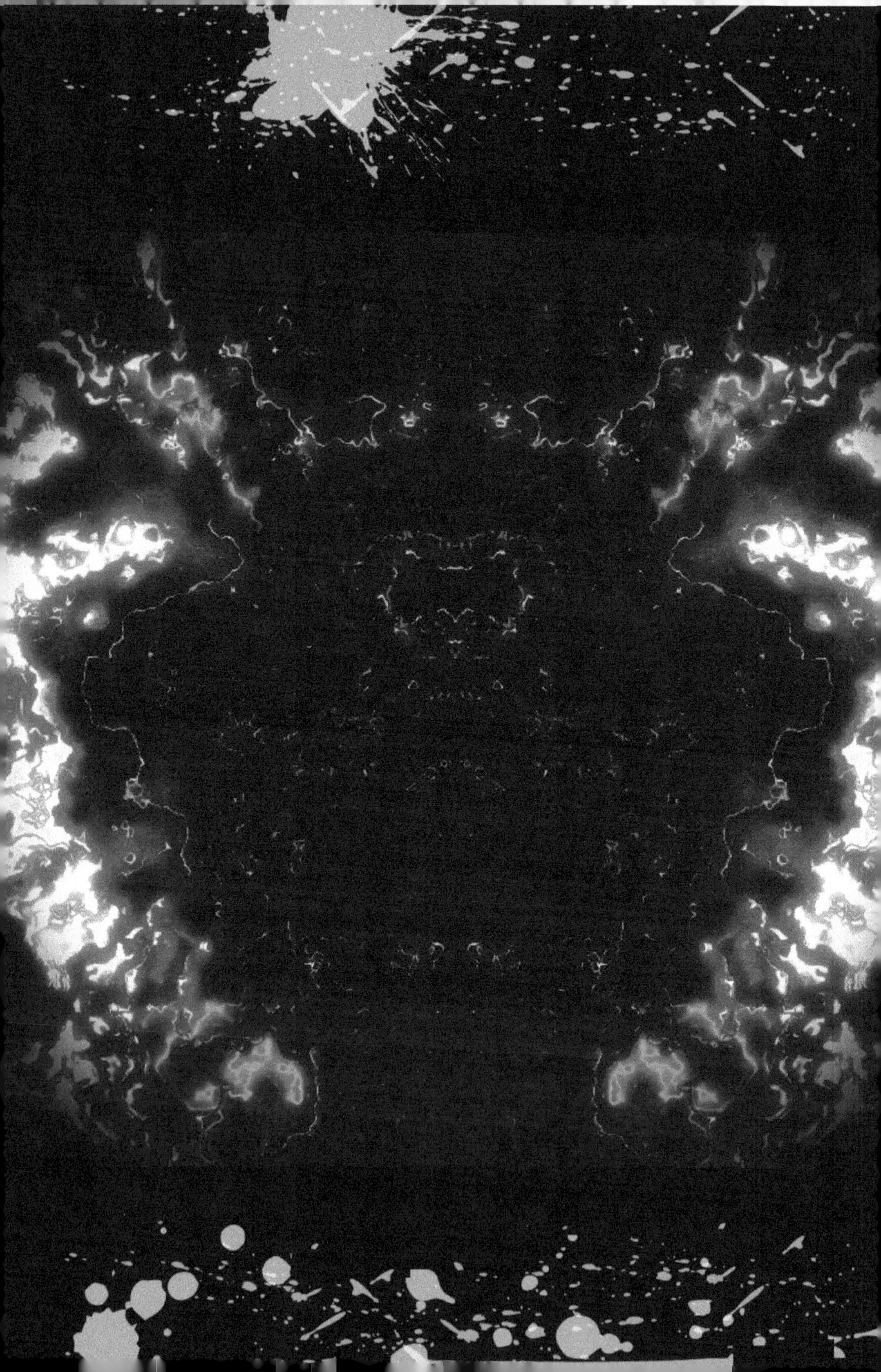

CYCLE OF MAGIC

The experience is unique.
When I throw ink onto the paper.
People will always label me a freak.
That's when the pace gets faster.
The ink runs slowly down the walls.
I've thrown many pens.
The monsters inside of me scream for it all...
Then I start over again.
A cycle of magic that I hope never ends.
It's like a machine.
The precision is tedious.
Like a never-ending dream where I rein victorious.
When I write the level of passion slaps the shit out of me.
It whips around its tentacles and from the page it leaps.
It creeps.
It screams!
Only it knows what I mean...

I'm screaming at myself again while crumbling this paper.
Those little fucking balls of shit do not mean shit to me!
Then I'll find myself digging through the trash.
Looking for that idea that I had.
Even though it's covered in maggots and putrid rotting lamb...
I grab it and open it fast.
There you are you son of a bitch!
I've inhaled too deep now the smell is making me sick.
Vomit everywhere.
New ideas are standing on my hairs.
My arms go numb then I start to write...

There is even vomit in my chair.
Writing is a nightmare.
Writing is the dream.
I'm writing out every echo within my silence that talks to me.

Do you think I'm crazy?
This cycle of magic will always be within me.

MELT

It drips so rapidly off of my hollow bones.
The echoes scream loudly throughout these catacombs.
There is nothing but pain here.
There is nothing but rage.
There are nothing but lost souls here searching for a way.
A way to understand why they are fucking here.
A way to make things finally come in clear…

The sounds that lurk here are merely static in the white noise.
The walls melt down and there is not a choice.
To embrace it.
To take it!
You can't blame it on anything here.
It knows each and every desire…
It knows each and every fear.
It then mixes them all together as it melts and disappears.
Over and over so residual.
Closer and closer as you feel so criminal.
Ravished again and again.
Lied to again and again.
You will be murdered as you melt again and again.
Between these melting walls there is never an exit.
There never was.
There never will be either.
No need to pray because there are no preachers.
This is the Devil's playground…
And you're it!
Look into that mirror and embrace your melting skin.
The pain was meant to be felt…
Again and again, you will relive your Hell…
Everything around you will continuously melt.

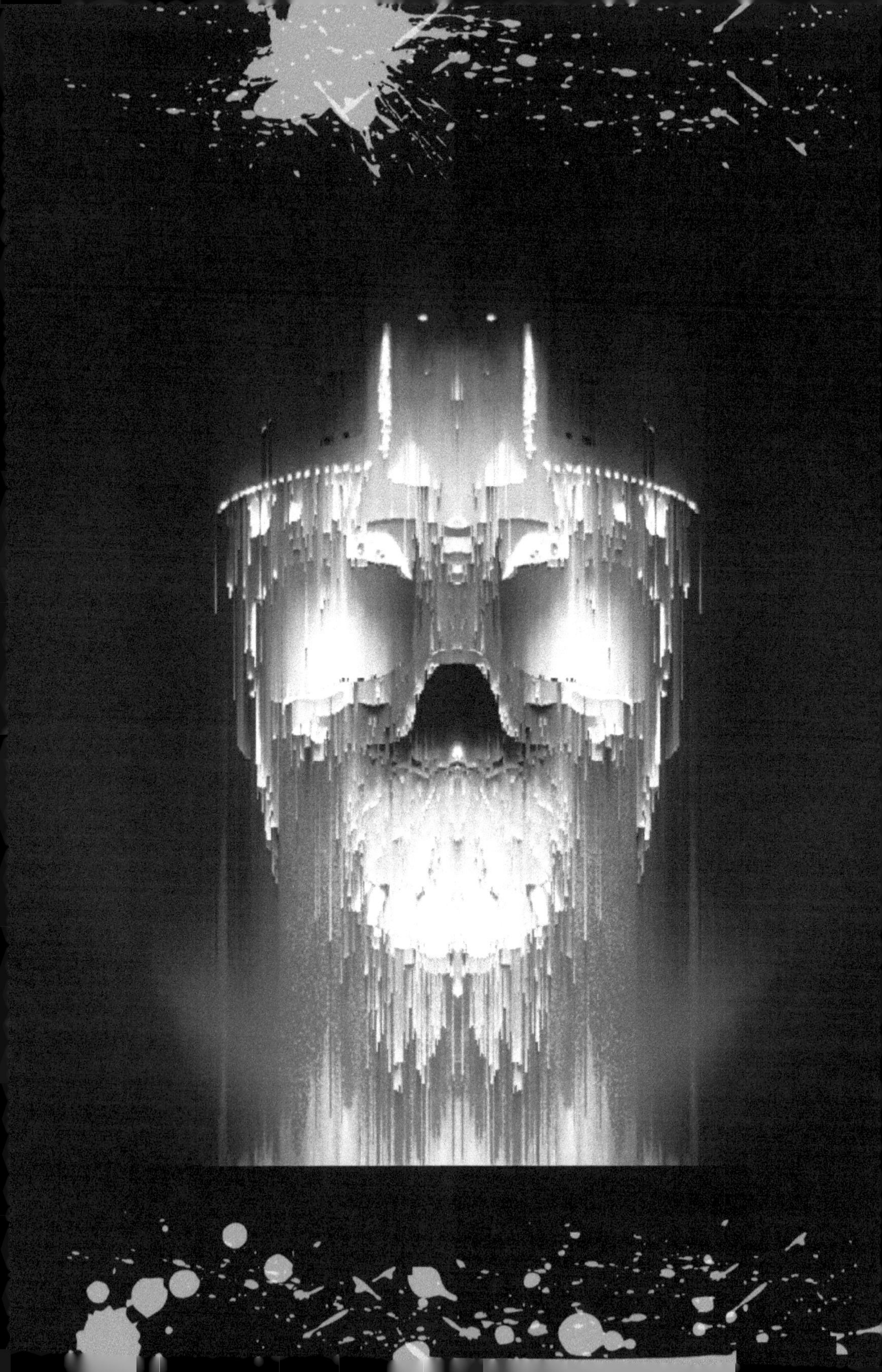

JUST A WEIRDO

I can't find how to be...
So normal.
They call me adorable.
When I cross the line.

I can't find how to feel.
The same way.
It hurts every day.
I can't break through.

I can't find what to say.
Without offending.
I'm incapable of pretending.
It's something that I just can't do.

When they tell me that I'm just a weirdo.
I smile as the tears shine through.
They are pointing and laughing right at me.
I'm complicated in everything that I do...

I can't find how to show...
The world that I'm trying.
Without denying.
As it cuts through.

I can't figure out how to run.
From each shadow.
From my ego.
It always tells me what to do.

I can't figure out how to shine.
In the darkness.
It treats me the harshest.
When it bites through.

When they tell me that I'm just a weirdo.
I smile as the tears shine through.
They are pointing and laughing right at me.
I'm complicated in everything that I do...

I'm just a weirdo...
How are you?

IT STARTS TO LEAK

The scratching becomes louder.
This happens every night.
I always smell a stench so sour.
I'm scrambling for the light.
Sounds of fingernails scraping down a chalkboard.
Sounds of lost souls dragging towards me like an undead horde.
I look at the wall.
It starts to leak.
That's when I know they are coming for me.
I can't scream!
I'm in a frozen state.
I want to throw up.
I can't even regurgitate.
Smells of death are rubbing into my face.
I'm ravished by the dead.
Every fucking night they laugh.
I can't take much more of this.
I am not supposed to squeal!
I must be out of my mind for real.
I'm so terrified of the walls when they start to leak...

When they start to scream I lose my shit.
When they start to bleed they take all of it.
They take my heart.
They take my soul.
They take my art.
They take my goals.
My ambitions dissolve and I am searching for where they go.
The walls hold secrets.

They absorb my dreams.
They never explain a fucking thing.
I put my fists through the walls when they start to leak.
Trying to prevent the madness that they inject into my being.
When the needles emerge so hollow and cold.
The fluid inside burns and leaks from my nose.
It is preparing me for the hell that awaits.
Once this happens there is no escape...
When the walls start to leak it's the end of the game.
When you hear the screaming echoes of what is contained...
Your soul has now been fucking claimed.
The walls have been leaking the blood from your own torturing
rage.

When the walls start to leak...
You better run the other way!

SORROW

We never know if we will wake up tomorrow.
Life will bring you unimaginable sorrow.
You have to go with the flow.
The rivers know how to inflict each blow.
It hits.
It hurts.
It stings and it burns!
Each second that passes is a lesson learned…

When sorrow takes the reins.
It whips and bruises your brain.
It's hard to escape a cage when it is filled with rage.
Sorrow creates a maze that you cannot navigate.
It changes in the process so you can never escape.
Your sorrow creates the pain.
Your sorrow creates the illusions that are always fucking fake.
It is not a place!
It is an emotion that you create.
It is a fire engulfed prison and the signs say one way.
If you turn back it stays the same.
If you go forward it opens the gates!
Your sorrow is not something that you should ever underestimate.
Your sorrow is how your demons lead your way.

REACHING FROM THE FIRE

People call me crazy.
As I go through life.
Tearing myself apart.
They just can't hear what screams at me in the dark.
The voices control what I do...
Always.

They call me crazy from what they think they see.
They don't know what's going on inside of me.

I'm reaching from the fire.
I'm reaching from the fire.

My eyes can get hazy.
I'm living in a fight.
Tearing out my own heart.
People never understand my work of art.
The voices control what I do...
Always.

They call me crazy from what they think they see.
They don't know what's going on inside of me.

I'm reaching from the fire.
I'm reaching from the fire.

I'm going through phases.
With teeth that bite.
Trying again to restart.

People will never understand why the hounds bark.
The voices control what I do...
Always.

They call me crazy from what they think they see.
They don't know what's going on inside of me.

I'm reaching from the fire.
I'm reaching from the fire.

FIGHT

I need a cure.
I need to find the door.
I need to search my soul again.
I need so much more.
I'm running for the shore.
My mind is so fucked up again.

I need to find a way to stop this abuse.
I need to find a way to escape my shattered youth.
All I need is love, you see.
I need to be assured.
I can't trust the words you say.
Because each one fucking burns.

I can't choose the correct door.
I need some help to find…
Because each way that I try to go.
I lose my fucking mind!

I need to light my fucking fuse.
I need to light it now.
I'm so tired of trying to figure myself out.
I know there has to be a way to turn the volume down.
I need to make sense of this fight.
I need to find my way to the light.
I need to make sense of this fight.

I need to find a way to stop this abuse.
I need to find a way to escape my shattered youth.

I don't know what I'm looking for.
I need to be assured.
I can't trust the words you say.
Because each one fucking burns!

I can't choose the correct door.
I need some help to find...
Because each way that I try to go.
I lose my fucking mind!

I need to light my fucking fuse.
I need to light it now.
I'm so tired of trying to figure myself out.
I know there has to be a way to turn the volume down.
I need to make sense of this fight.
I need to find my way to the light...
I need to make sense of this fight!

My blood is on the walls.
I have lost it all!
The illusions never end.
My soul I must defend...

I need to find a way to stop this abuse.
I need to find a way to escape my shattered youth.
I don't know what I'm looking for.
I need to be assured.
I can't trust the words you say.
Because each one fucking burns!

I need to make sense of this fight...

CATTLE KING

Listen closely if you value your life.
Open your ears and follow me into the night.
There will be no pity in the heat of the flames.
The demons do not care about your fucking birth name.
You will be the cattle as each one is laughing.
You will be the cattle king.
You will hear your broken heart beat so fastly...
As you scream from your knees!

Your new name is the cattle king.
The meat you will bring.
You are the feast.
You've met the beast.
You are the cattle king.
Moo!

Take a look into that mirror you hate.
Take a glance into your incoming fate.
Watch the omens arise from their deep putrid graves.
This is the place that your soul has made.
When the flesh is ripped away from your carcass.
You'll scream into fright.
When your soul descends into your darkness...
You better fight for your life!

Your new name is the cattle king.
The meat you will bring.
You are the feast.
You've met the beast.

You are the cattle king.
Moo!

You're in a place of hate.
You're in the place you fear.
You're in the place that made you...
You're in the place that your meat will sear!

Your new name is the cattle king.
The meat you will bring.
You are the feast.
You've met the beast.
You are the cattle king.
Moo!

Listen closely if you value your life.
Open your ears and follow me into the night.

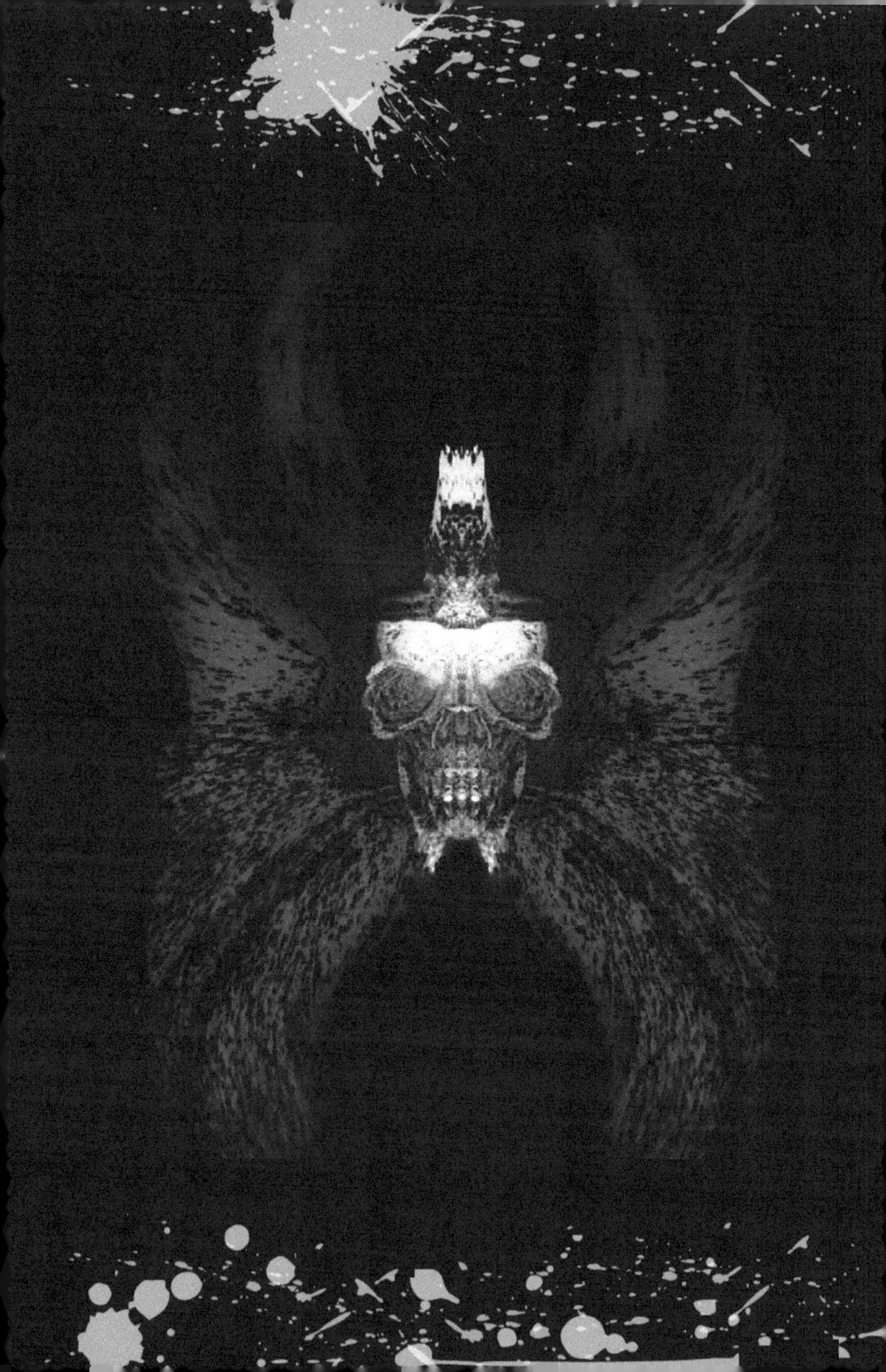

HOME

I've opened many doors.
What was behind each one I was never sure.
I was turned into a whore...
Within the darkness that I was so desperate to explore.
This place was always fake.
This place was designed to fucking take...
Everything away that you create.
Once you sign the contract the deal has been made.

Inside of the place that always takes away your dreams.
You're building a home that you call a masterpiece.
In here the pleasure covers up your many screams.
You will never be able to run away.

You are stuck here.
You are caged.
You are stuck here...
In your own fucking rage!

When I stepped into the void.
I really didn't have a fucking choice.
I followed the white noise.
I followed that demon's beautiful voice.
I knew what was at stake.
When I signed the dotted line that sealed my fate.
It had my soul to take.
I just gave it the fuck away!

Inside of the place that always takes away your dreams.

You're building a home that you call a masterpiece.
In here the pleasure covers up your screams.
You will never be able to run away.

You are stuck here.
You are caged.
You are stuck here...
In your own fucking rage!

When I stepped into the void...
I really didn't have a fucking choice.

HUNTED BY THE SUN

I'm hiding my soul again.
It's lost deep within my nightmares.
I'm hiding within my dreams again.
They will never end.
I am looking for sweet relief.
Deep within my madness.
I am called a creep...
I scream into the night!

There is no place to go.
There is nowhere to run.
I'm being hunted by the sun.
The burns upon my skin.
Are my many gifts.
What I've done can't be undone.
I can't run!

The ultraviolet rays.
I am tattooing my soul now.
I have a price to pay.
I will pay with many scars.
Look deep into me.
You will not find my heart beating.
It exploded long ago...
It's splattered on the walls.

There is no place to go.
There is nowhere to run.
I'm being hunted by the sun.

The burns upon my skin.
Are my many gifts.
What I've done can't be undone.
I can't run.
I can't run.
I can't run!

The burns can't be undone.
There are so many more to come...
I'm being hunted by the sun!

I can't run!

FALLING ON MY ASS

My heart feels so alone.
Like it has turned to stone.
I'll never find my home...
I'm dying to get a hold of it.
This life has cut me out.
I'm an outcast that plays with the hounds.
They came up out of the ground...
Snarling while attacking me.

I can't find my place.
There are just too many mistakes.
I'm floating face down in this lake...
The lake is engulfed in flames.
I can't do anything but shout.
As the fire burns me down.
There are hands reaching out...
Pulling me into my misery.

I am falling on my ass.
Shattering the glass.
Trying to find myself but I'm falling too fast.
Reaching for the man that I used to be.
I can't find him.

I am falling on my ass.
As the hounds attack.
I can't find my way I'm on the wrong fucking path.
I'll never be the man that I used to be...
I can't find him!

I've lost my soul again.
This cycle never ends.
I've lost most everything...
I need to find my way again.
I'm screaming with an open mouth.
I'm frozen in fear and doubt.
Nothing really matters now.
So cold as I'm shivering.

I am falling on my ass.
Shattering the glass.
Trying to find myself but I'm falling too fast.
Reaching for the man that I used to be.
I can't find him.

I am falling on my ass.
My wrists are cut open on the shattered glass.
I can't find my way I'm on the wrong fucking path.
I'll never be the man that I used to be...
I can't find him!

I'm falling on my ass!

DANCE ON THE DECAY

We are all out of our minds in some kind of way.
The faces within the shadows change as the fire creates the
imaginary rain.
We can't determine if it is night or day.
In the place where you dance on the decay...

There are no right turns here.
There are no left turns either.
Everything continues in a circle forever.
Nothing will ever come in clearer.
It tricks you into thinking everything will be okay.
In the end you will still dance on the decay.

In a place that calls your forgotten name.
A place designed to take it away.
You will always burn in its flames.
As you dance on the decay.
The smell of rot won't go away.
The monsters will always want to play.
You will never find your way as you dance on the decay.

In this place where...
You lose your soul, it's a nightmare.
You're starving and sick!
The shadows take you!
The shadows take you!
You can't get out...
In a sea of shouts, you're a lost soul!
You're a lost soul!

Nobody will ever hear your soul scream...

In a place that calls your forgotten name.
A place designed to take it away.
You will always burn in its flames.
As you dance on the decay.
The smell of rot won't go away.
The monsters will always want to play.
You will never find your way as you dance on the decay.
You were always still in this place!!!

It told you everything was going to be okay.
As you danced beautifully on the decay.
The rotting corpses called your name.
As they opened up your grave.
You weren't supposed to find your way.
You have found your price to pay.
They've been lying here in wait...
While you danced on the decay.

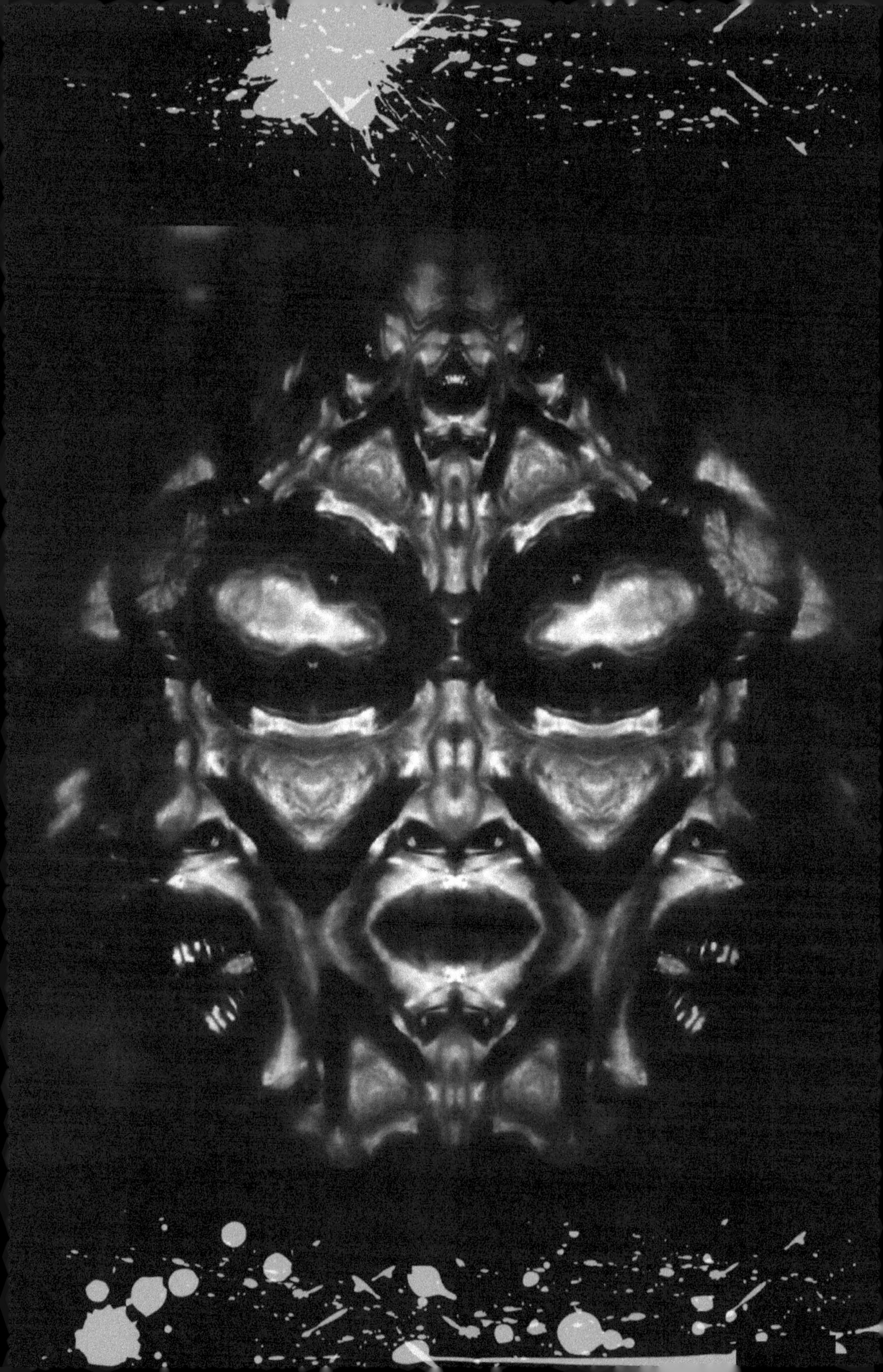

NEWBORN MAGGOTS

My vivid dreams are crashing.
They are telling lies.
Each one goes on like an echo.
Just let me scream.
Some dreams are hollow.
Wherever I go...
Please do not follow...

My dreams hurt.
My dreams heal.
My dreams burn.
My dreams squeal.
You wouldn't last.
You wouldn't make it.
You would shatter in the glass.
Your bones would break into pieces.
My thoughts are not chosen.
My thoughts are forced.
Inside of my mind is broken.
It's so easy to change course.
I'm pacing inside of a madness that is beyond intense.
The funnel clouds are colorful in their winds of regret.
The shadows are unpredictable as each one is met.
Some shadows will tear off your face.
Some shadows will rip open your chest.
In madness there is no right or left.
In madness there is no political nonsense.
I do not care about blue and red.
Make sense?

Get over yourselves.
The newborn maggots consume us all in the end.

My vivid dreams are crashing.
They are telling lies.
Each one goes on like an echo.
Just let me scream.
Some dreams are hollow.
Wherever I go...
Please do not follow...

Stop the lies and pretend...
The newborn maggots consume us all in the end.

THE KNIFE DRAGS DOWN

This is how insanity starts.
The knife drags down.
Please don't cut me deeper.
I'm so tired of my soul leaking out.

I've fought many battles that you wouldn't understand.
I've seen many things that have claws instead of hands.
I've set many doors on fire that were not intended for me.
I've opened many wounds that I didn't want the world to see.
Shadows are dangerous.
You must be careful how you walk.
Hell will make you famous while cutting out your tongue.
I never said that I was the greatest.
That is not what I said at all.
I did say that I know what it's like to stumble and fall.
I did say that my knuckles are scarred up from beating on the walls.
You don't seem to understand anything that's crumbled on those
little paper balls.
The ones I scatter at my feet.
They all contain a dream.
They all contain a scream.
They all contain a different beast.
Understand me or don't.
I was never intended to be explained.
I'm force fed these words.
Then I vomit on each page.

If you wanted to know more about me all you had to do was ask.
If you assume that you know everything it will put you on your ass.

Pointing your fingers within darkness will quickly get you trapped.
The sounds are now echoing from your torturing past.
The pages will always pile higher in little balls on the floor.
If you're too scared to see what's written on them…
I suggest you don't open those doors.
Blow the dust off of that cover if you would like to know more.

This is how insanity starts.
The knife drags down.
Please don't cut me deeper.
I'm so tired of my soul leaking out.

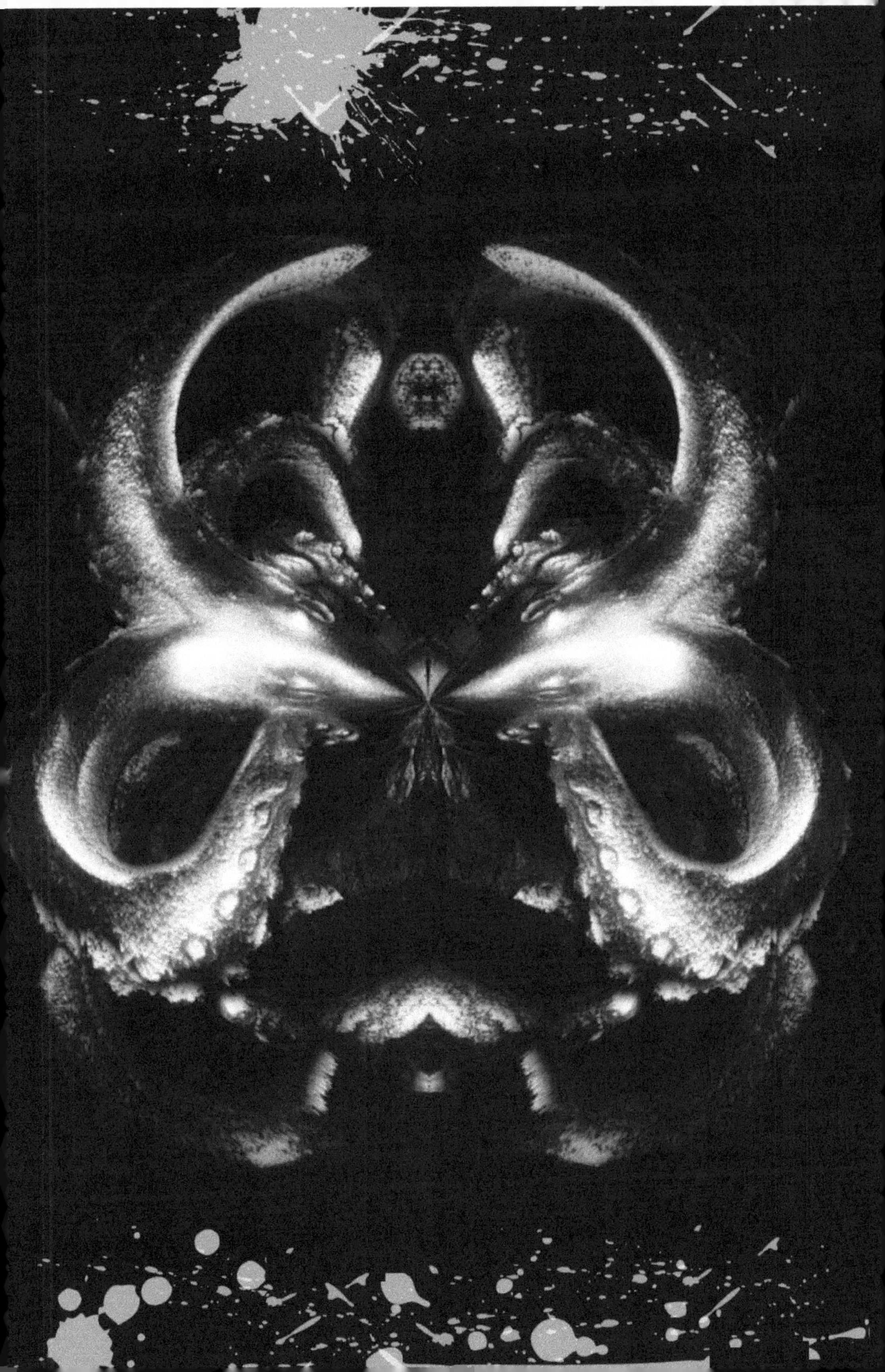

WONDER

I am not alone out here on this cruel prison called earth.
The only way out is the death of us...
This planet has always been cursed.
There are hidden messages within the ocean waves.
There are messages that are not hidden too...
They are lined beneath the graves.
Painted and splashed in blood all over the hallowed grounds.
If you place your ear on the soil you can hear them moving around.
I wonder what they do down there...
I wonder about their conversations.
I wonder how much is lost when we die.
I wonder how much is taken.
I wonder if there really is Heaven and Hell.
I wonder about many things.
Tonight I placed my ear to the ground.
All that I heard were screams.
I never intended to know what they mean.
I just wanted to learn more.
I think I'm taking in more than I can handle...
And I can't handle much more.

I am tired of wondering if I can finally heal.
I am tired of wondering as I'm spinning this wheel.
I wonder if death is the same as life.
I wonder if the maggots and worms are nice.
Above the soil all that this world gives is pain.
I wonder if it's beautiful beneath the grave.
I wonder if in death I can finally find my place.
I wonder...

INKBLOTS

No Doctor!
I don't want to look at the cards.
It only resurfaces my many buried scars.
The ones I can't carry for all to see.
Why aren't you listening to me?
I'm trying to explain.
If I look at the inkblots, I will not be able to be contained...

He then pulled them out anyway.
He started saying my name.
What does this look like?
Do you see colors or shapes?
I can't look at these!
I know what's going to happen.
I'm going to start freaking out and delivering pain.
The colors and shapes!
The inkblots make me crazed!
I think it's done on purpose to keep me caged.
I'm starting to seize.
The convulsions are happening.
It is just the beginning.
Just wait until I start laughing.

There is a darkness that awakens when I stare at the inkblots.
The walls turn to fire.
I start seeing coal black dots.
Each one gives a different instruction.
I am being played like a game...
They hit all of the right buttons.

I'm no longer in control of myself.
I am no longer sitting at the helm.

Whatever they tell me to do...
I do.
I feel bad for the Doctor holding the cards right now asking me if I
can see blue.

SHAPES

Look into your own eyes.
Gaze into your reflection for a while.
The shapes will always shift as you emerge from a beautiful denial.
The colors change like the changing of the leaves on a cold autumn
night.
You can hear each creature chattering but there is not a monster in
sight.
They are noisy while they hide.
They want to keep you out of your mind.
You can hear their teeth grind!
The shapes shift at all times.
Within the screaming confines of your torn apart mind.

Stop the shapes from shifting.
I'm losing my head.
I'm so tired of pretending.
My soul is almost dead.
I'm running out of energy.
I've been running my entire life.
From the shadows that consume me.
From the insidious demons that bite.
I can't run any longer.
From the shapes that draw blood.
I can't breathe much longer.
In this incoming flood.
I'm almost done.
The shapes have overcome the heart within me.
There's blood on the ground.
There's blood on the trees.
The shapes have consumed me!

DEMON OF THE HEART

Her horns are in the shape of a heart.
If you're brave enough to realize this.
You'll spot it from the start.
You have to look directly into her luring light.
She will seduce you in many ways.
She will force her pleasure into your mortal veins...

The demon of the heart can take many forms.
It can beautifully paint your deepest desires...
While painting so much more.
Then it spits fire into your face.
Sitting on your chest while you rot away.
It's laughing!
You better bet your ass it is.
It has you right where it wants you...
It is in desperate need of a fix.
It will stop at nothing to get it.
Let me repeat...
It will stop at nothing to get it.

The demon of the heart always wins...
It then chooses your immortality.

THAT'S WHERE THE FIRE STARTS

I'd love to visit the moon.
I'd love to fly within the stars.
I'd love to be away from the place that always breaks my heart.
Even if just for a moment...
I'd love to be that far.
There'd be nothing like just being at peace...
Just long enough to heal the scars.
I go out of tune.
I go way off the charts.
I go away to a place that is made of glass and broken shards.

Even if just for a moment.
I'd love to be that far.
There'd be nothing like just being at ease...
So the memories can't tear me apart.

I swim out to find the stars above.
I look beyond the sky...
In this place that cuts me deep I've never been this high.
Let's find out what happens here.
We don't have much time.
I tune out when the ocean salt fills in my lungs.
I tune out when the shadows talk.
I tune out when the creatures walk.
I tune out, the demons are holding chalk!
The outline of my madness has just begun!

I tune all the way out.
I can't control my tortured heart.

I leave my body deep down in the gutter
That's where the fire starts...
That's where I create my art.
That's where I can't see shit while trying to count each star.
I love to be this far...

That's where the fire starts.

WATCHING INK RUN

As I watch each blot of ink run.
Changing faces and loading my gun.
I can't find the light of the sun.
My open wounds are bleeding faster.
I can't keep an open mind!
This place has no concept of time.

I'm watching ink run.
I'm spinning this gun.
I'm trying to take this pain away.
I'm losing touch.
This is too much.
I have no more words to say.

In the darkness I can see my face.
Changing colors and rotting away.
Just like when the seasons change.
My open wounds are bleeding faster.
I can't keep an open mind!
This place has no concept of time.

I'm watching ink run.
I'm spinning this gun.
I'm trying to take this pain away.
I'm losing touch.
This is too much.
I have no more words to say.

The blots of ink now take the place.

Of the blood that I have wasted.
I can't find the perfect pace.
My mind and soul are perfectly jaded.
What is left for me to do?
I'm lost in darkness and so confused.

I'm watching ink run.
I'm spinning this gun.
I'm trying to take this pain away.
I'm losing touch.
This is too much.
I have no more words to say.

How can I ever find the truth?
If this place is complicated.
All that lurks here is my abuse.
As my open wounds keep bleeding faster...
I still can't keep an open mind!
This place will never have a concept of time.

I'm watching ink run.
I'm spinning this gun.
I'm trying to take this pain away.
I'm losing touch.
This is too much.
I have no more words to say...
I'm watching ink run.

BONES

I've been trapped within this darkness for as long as I can
remember.
I can't find the door that will put the pieces back together.
I can't find my voice.
I do not have a choice.
My ears are bleeding profusely from the soul crushing noise.
The bottomless pit has sucked me into the void.
There is nothing to see here.
Please move right along.
Hell has its own conductor...
Hell has its own songs.
If you listen close enough it will show you where you belong.

The fire is relentless as it rips your skin away.
Exposing the bones underneath that will never decay.
You will then watch your entire shell melt entirely away.
You're now just a pile of bones left to scream in pain...
Then the reanimation begins again and again.
Your skin then will return to your bones.
Melting off of you for an eternity...
Returning again.
A blistering cycle that will never fucking end.
The melodies will play forever for you to enjoy.
As you scream again and again into the fire filled void.

HOURS

There are many exploding emotions.
They flow through me like hourglass sand.
My thoughts always race so rampant.
Ink stays stained on my hands.
There are hours of fighting myself.
There are hours of fighting my demons.
There are hours of writing out my Hell.
There are hours of thinking of reasons.
When I fight myself I'm frantic.
When I fight myself I'm manic.
When I'm writing in Hell I panic.
When I'm thinking of reasons the words get sporadic.
I'm scratching words into paper like a brilliant maniac...
This and that.
That and this.
Lean over into my darkness where it will make you sick.
Come inside and feel the fire that burns me to a crisp.

What happens when I fight for my soul?

All of the above will mix.

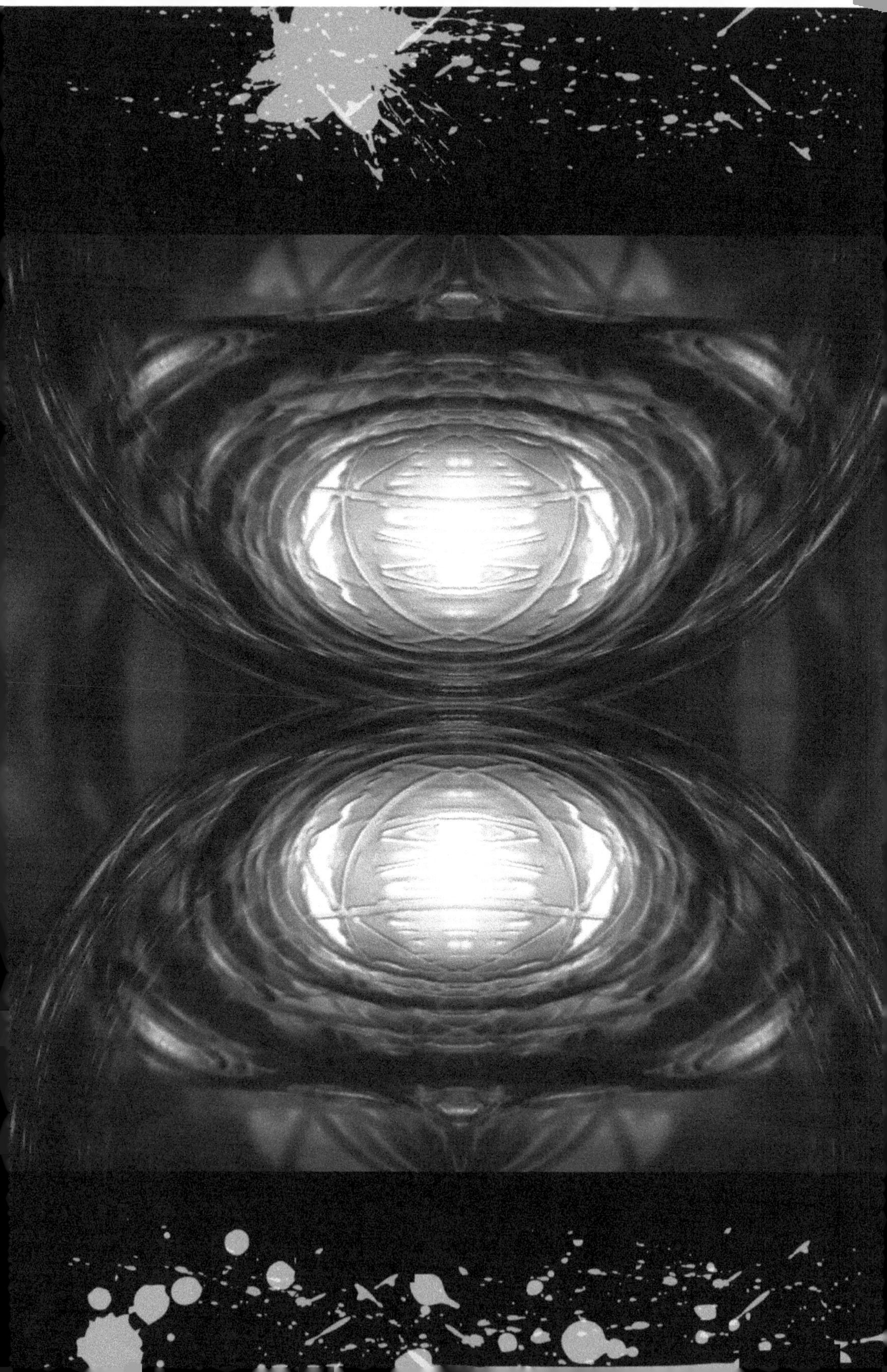

WELCOME TO HELL

What kind of pain can you bear?
This is not a nightmare.
I'm walking these streets in the dangerous parts.
This I am fully aware of.

What kind of soul have you got?
I hope you're ready to rot.
I'm walking these hallways with flames all around.
I have to take my fucking shot.

Welcome to Hell...
It's not what you've imagined.
I bet it doesn't make too much sense.

Welcome to Hell.
Full of Demons and Savages...
They haven't been eating too well.

You must know how to navigate.
This won't be easy to complete.
Your soul is on the line...
And you don't have much time before you become a part of the
feast.

You must know how to find your way.
The maze will change with the beat.
With the beating of your heart and the depth of your scars...
Are you ready to meet the beast?

Welcome to Hell...
It's not what you've imagined.
I bet it doesn't make too much sense.

Welcome to Hell.
Full of Demons and Savages...
They haven't been eating too well.

What kind of pain can you bear?
What kind of soul have you got?
You must find your own way out of the flare...
You're here whether you like it or not.

CLIPBOARD

Madness illustrates what it demonstrates.
Chaos illuminates what your own personal Hell creates.
There is so much at stake but you're not even aware...
You're not aware of what is really waiting for you down there.

You're blind to it because you refuse to believe it.
You're science minded and you have to fucking see it.
In your mind I'm out of mine...
I see visions that are not mine.
I can't tell the fucking time when it keeps switching from day to
night.
Use your fucking logic and tell me how to stop it!
I'm waiting to hear how you will stop something demonic.
You still won't believe me.
Look at the claw marks on my skin...
Does that look fucking human inflicted?
You still blame me and say I did it to myself.
You still write on your little fucking clipboard and won't tell.
You still let me burn away in this place!
Without your help I can never escape...

Madness illustrates what it demonstrates.
Chaos illuminates what your own personal Hell creates.
There is so much at stake but you're not even aware...
You're not aware of what is really waiting for you down there.

I don't even think you're writing anything down on that useless
clipboard.
I don't even think you can handle the truth and what it has in store.

I'm watching you scribble away as you refuse to listen to me anymore.
They are coming from the flames.
They will make us pay.
I need your hand to pull me out of the fire!
You just sit there and continue to fake...
Your way through existence as another soul is taken.
You refuse to believe it because your vision has been forsaken.
You can't even hear my chainsaw cranking!
Better run Doctor!
You are mine for the taking...

Madness illustrates what it demonstrates.
Chaos illuminates what your own personal Hell creates.
There is so much at stake but you're not even aware...
You're not aware of what is really waiting for you down there.

The clipboard is in pieces now...
I'm dying to see what was written down.

SHINE

It's hard out here in the darkness.
Yet there is so much room for all of us to shine.
I know life can treat you the harshest.
I've been to that place many times.
It is all about technique.
It is all about how you walk through Hell's fake masterpiece.
You have to dream through it.
You have to scream through it.
You must find your immunity as you bleed through it.
There are no shortcuts.
But there are many hidden doors.
You see your flesh melt off within the mirror...
You feel the pain even more.
The illusion of the fire has so much more than that in store.
You must walk barefoot through the broken glass.
Then you may pass on to explore.
What you will find is beyond any logical explanation.
I wouldn't even try to find one.
You'll be digging holes for the rest of your life...
You'll never find that imaginary gun.
It doesn't exist.
It was planted in your thoughts to trick you.
Make a wish.
Nothing here will protect you.
You have to navigate your own special path.
You have to pay attention to the shadows as they laugh.
You have to memorize every paralyzing sound...
You have to listen while being hunted down.
Use your eyes even when you're blind.

It's hard out here in the darkness.
Yet there is so much room for all of us to shine....

GREED MEANS MORE

Why do some people think that they can put others down?
This question has never been really answered.
I'm about to tell a little story about why I do not give a fuck...
Enjoy it or skip it.
It really doesn't matter.

What you say about me is none of my concern.
The pettiness and the childish drama will always get you burned.
Leave it right by the door before you enter here.
It has no meaning where my mind is eternally clear.
I've evolved from bullshit.
I've evolved from mind games.
The ignorant will call me selfish when I call them out by name.
They don't like it when somebody puts them in their place.
They don't like to get dirty...
You won't see a spec of dirt on their face.
Clean cut and silver spoon fed.
Never had to work hard for anything that they have.
They just act like it.
They talk about their hardships...
When the reality of their entire existence is literally Bull Shit.
They then have the nerve to treat others like garbage.

I do not care how rich you are.
I do not care how many fans you have.
I do not care about your one hundred thousand dollar car.
I do not care if this makes you mad.
You didn't work for it...
It was placed in your hand.

Do not tell me that you fucking understand.
This might sound like I'm hating.
That's all fine and good.
I'm simply demonstrating reality to these jokers so I am completely understood.
If every millionaire and billionaire on this planet came together...
They could end child poverty.
They could end homelessness.
They could solve every problem that totally annihilates the poor.
They hold on to it though...
Because their greed means more...

All about me.
All about my clique.
All about preaching things that I don't live for.
All about money.
All about myself.
All about what I can do...
Throw those peasants into the well.

They leave us to burn into their creation of Hell...
Leaving us with nothing while they eat so well.

And that my friends is why I do not give a fuck!

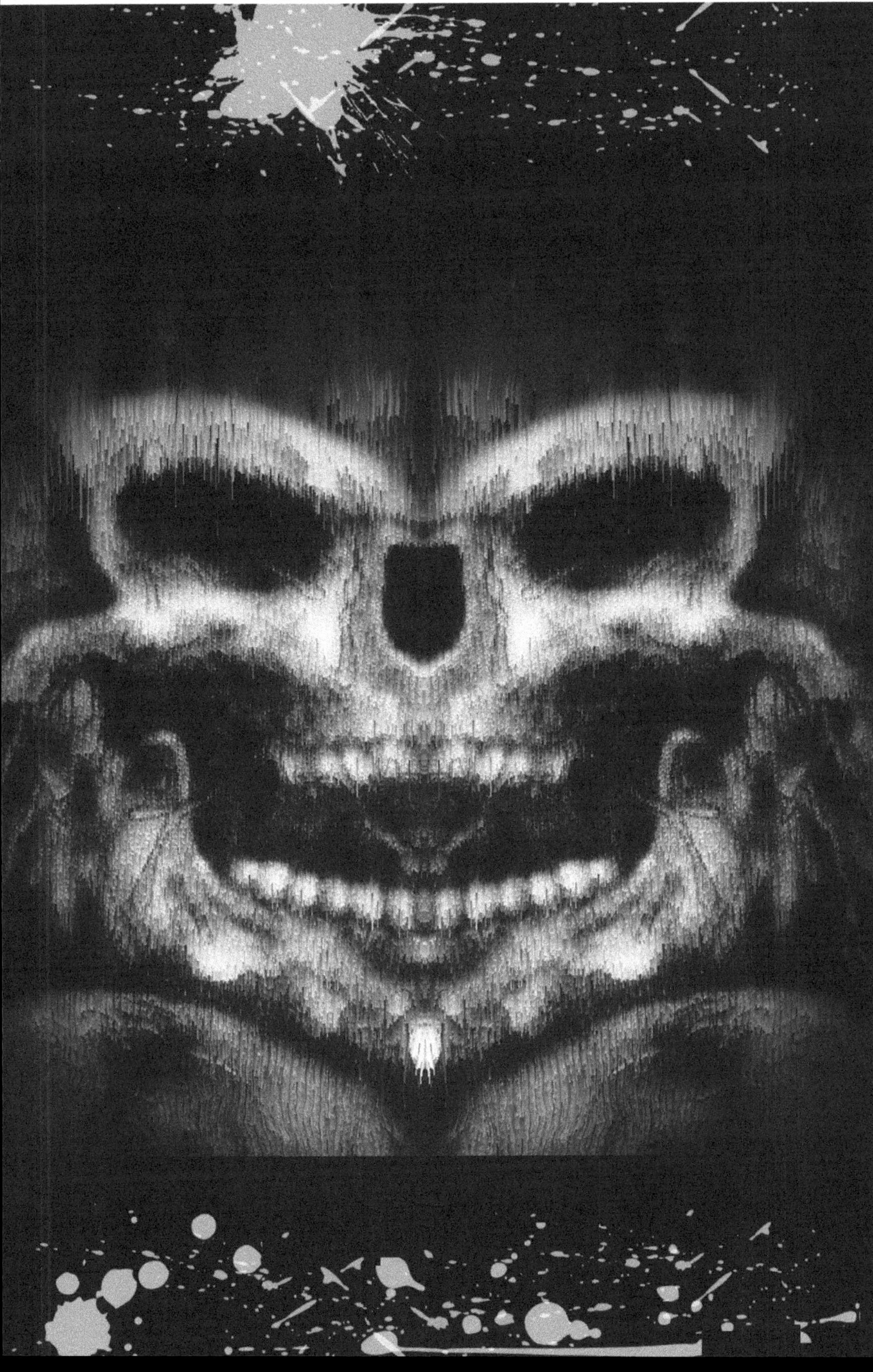

THEY WILL FORGET YOU

The shadows are talking everywhere around me.
They have an agenda to tear my mind apart.
After a while your loved ones can't understand you.
Leaving you alone until the day that you die.

They will forget you...
As you scream from the walls.
They won't protect you.
They never loved you at all.

When you look into their eyes they will no longer see you.
Only the insanity that you are forced to have.
They can't understand and they'll never try to.
They throw away the key and leave your soul so mad.

They will forget you...
As you scream from the walls.
They won't protect you.
They never loved you at all.

You look through the window as they drive away.
Watching your whole world light up on the tailgate.
They left you because they thought you were crazy.
Leaving you to waste right where you are...

They will forget you...
As you scream from the walls.
They won't protect you.
They never loved you at all.
They never loved you at all...

LOST BOY

Hello again.
I've missed you my friend.
Have you been hiding within the shadows again?
I've searched everywhere for you...
Where have you been?
I can't live without you my fire filled friend...

In the darkness I don't feel so alone.
When I hold your hand my heart turns to stone.
In the fire I don't feel like a lost boy on my own.
The cobblestone path that leads to the grey gates leads to the beast that sits on its throne.
My home away from home burns me into a person that you've never known.
My eyes fill with fire.
My aggression becomes higher.
I can feel my demons inside of me as they fucking conspire.
I know they are liars.
I know what they desire.
They desire that this lost boy to enter the gray gates of fire.
I've already entered long ago.
I've listened closely to each of the shadows.
There is nowhere else for me to go.
I'm just that lost boy in hell that craves that fucking throne.

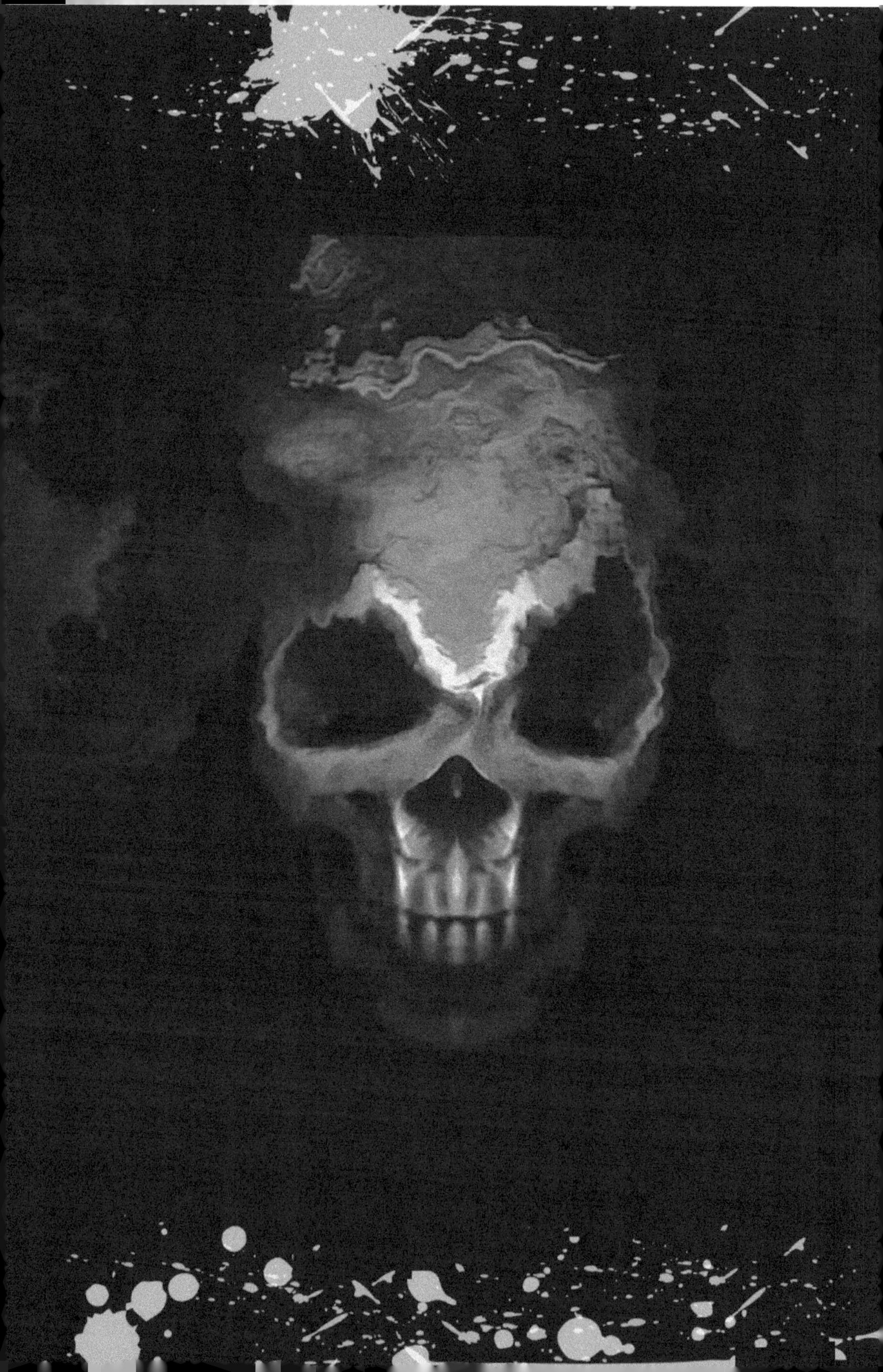

I TELL MYSELF

I tell myself that I'm going to pull through this.
They don't see it like I see it; they see nothing at all.
I tell myself that I'm going to escape this darkness.
As I'm counting the many holes that I've punched in my walls.
I can't remember what the Doctor said.
So much for my heart...
It is now dead.

I tell the voices that keep calling my name.
That I can no longer listen to the words that they have to say.
I have had enough of their fucking torture I can't take much more
pain.
I won't take them to my grave.
Right here is where they will stay.
Frozen ink on the paper where they will forever lay.
I can't take much more today...
So I'm throwing the voices away!

I can't load this gun.
I can't overcome it.
My soul is on the run.
I can't take this!
I'm walking a fine line.
My moods switch on a dime.
I know I don't have much time...
I will soon be crossing the divide.
Where the demons thrive.
Where the Angels sing.
Where my soul can't hide.

Where the light burns out my eyes.
It is where I'll find the answers I couldn't find while alive.

I tell myself that I'm going to pull through this.
They don't see it like I see it; they see nothing at all.
I tell myself that I'm going to escape this darkness.
As I'm counting the many holes that I've punched in my walls.

TRASH

The shards of glass impale.
The pain is so intense.
I don't want this to make sense.
I've given this everything I have...
Then it was ripped away.

The memories fall like ash.
The thoughts then cut so deep.
I am screaming to be released!
There is not a chance for me...
I cannot leave.

I thought this was over...
I thought this shit would get better!

I can't control you but I adore you.
I can't get you out of me.
I thought I fixed this.
Changed this.
That's what you had me believe.
You told me that you loved me.
Then you cut me.
You left me here to bleed.

If I knew the truth.
It would never be this way.

You were a part of my soul.
You were a part of me.

Then you released me into the trees.
You were everything that I ever needed...
Then you ripped it away.

I'm now forced into the past.
Cutting my skin on the broken glass.
Looking for you through the trash.
I never wanted things this way...
What else can I say?

I thought this was over...
I thought this shit would get better!

I can't control you but I adore you.
I can't get you out of me.
I thought I fixed this.
Changed this.
That's what you had me believe.
You told me that you loved me.
Then you cut me.
You left me here to bleed.

If I knew the truth.
There would never be this pain.
I never wanted things this way...
What else can I say?

I'll be here in the past...
Searching for you through the trash.

BENEATH THE GRAVE

When you die make sure they remember your name.
You don't want to be just another rotting corpse beneath the grave.
Create your place in history no matter how small it may be.
Leave a mark that matters for the rest of eternity.
We don't have very long to write our breathing stories.
We only have so many years to create the inventory.
Be humble.
Work hard.
Lose yourself within your chaos as you grab each burning star.
Once you're beneath the grave all of that is gone.
We are living to die.
We are living to get by.
We are scurrying rats with different colored eyes.
Beneath the grave leaves nothing left alive...

You must leave that all behind.

ONLY A GHOST

Watch me fly so high above.
Watch my lungs fill up with salt.
Watch the ocean pull me right down.
Listen for me there are no sounds.

When you reached for me it was far too late.
You knew for so long what was at stake.
You left me here to drown alone.
You left me here to die so cold.

I am only a ghost that is trying to go home.
You could have saved me so long ago.
I am only a ghost.
I am your shadow.
Why didn't you save me so long ago?

So long ago...

I will be here in your dreams.
You left me there to drown and scream.
Let me show you just how it felt.
Let me show you my residual Hell.

I will haunt your every move.
I have nothing left to prove.
You will hear me screaming in your ears.
You will see your darkest fears...

I am only a ghost that is trying to go home.

You could have saved me so long ago.
I am only a ghost.
I am your shadow.
Why didn't you save me so long ago?

So long ago...

I'm holding you under the ocean tides.
In the same place you left me to die.
I am holding you down as the salt burns your eyes.
You cannot scream as it masks your cries.

My revenge has come to pass.
Now you can join me within the oceans mass.
Endless waters for us to explore.
You can join me forever...
Forevermore.

I am only a ghost that is trying to go home.
You could have saved me so long ago.
I am only a ghost.
I am your shadow.
Why didn't you save me so long ago?
So long ago...

I'VE LOST

There's something in this place that I can't hold together.
It hits me.
It haunts me.
It opens me up as my skin begins to sever.
It falls off of me.
It abuses me.

It won't let up until the day that I surrender.
It taunts me.
It tricks me.
With one eye closed I can't sleep in this kind of weather.
The waves pound me and surround me.

It's where I've always been.
With the voices in my head.

Surrounding me.
Pounding me into someone that I can't force myself to take.

I've lost my way again.
I've lost the will to win.

Surrounding me.
Pounding me into someone that I can't force myself to take.

There's something in this place that wants to pull me under.
It calls me.
It wants me.
It gives me my desires as they are masked by the rolling thunder.

It deafens me.
It sickens me.

It confuses my free will and leaves me here to wonder.
It deceives me.
It needs me.
It fucks me within my soul and then leaves me in the gutter.
The garbage piles around me and becomes me.

It's where I've always been.
With the voices in my head.

Surrounding me.
Pounding me into someone that I can't force myself to take.

I've lost my way again.
I've lost the will to win.

Surrounding me.
Pounding me into someone that I can't force myself to take.

I've Lost...

HERE YOU CAN SING

I find myself within the eye of the storm.
It is the place where my soul is reborn.
The world will show no mercy as I fall for its lies.
I'm stuck in purgatory where the demons reach high...

They are reaching for a soul to take now.
They don't care who you are.
What you did in life will never matter...
In a place that is so foul.

Here you can sing.
Here your ears ring.
The leader awaits in the flames.
You have dug your own grave.
Here you can sing...
Sing!

In this place you watch your soul slowly die.
You will dissolve in the storm's massive eye.
The glass shatters in the mess you have made.
The clock has stopped ticking as you always deny...

You deny everything that swirls around you.
Nothing is ever your fault.
You deny the ones that tried to save you.
Now you are hitting the walls!

Here you can sing.
Here your ears ring.

The leader awaits in the flames.
You have dug your own grave.
Here you can sing...
Sing!

In the silence that you fear.
You can hear the monsters clearly.
You now watch yourself disappear...
You can sing right the fuck along!

Here you can sing.
Here your ears ring.
The leader awaits in the flames.
You have dug your own grave.
Here you can sing...
Sing!

In the eye of that storm.
You hear a familiar song.
You are once again reborn.
You are where your soul belongs...

Here you can sing...
Sing!

ALONE

The shadows sing me their lullabies.
It is not the ones that you think.
It sings me the songs…
Of the damned and the gone.
And I can't rise up from my knees.

They sing to me so softly.
Then both of my ear drums explode.
The pitch of their melodies reminds me so suddenly…
That I will never go home.

I'm screaming in the darkness alone.
I'm screaming in the darkness alone.

They then open my chest up for surgery.
I can see my own beating heart.
The screams are induced so perfectly…
This Hell has no shining stars.

When my heart was ripped out.
I could not scream and shout.
Then the pain played again and again.
I then knew I'd be here forever with my many demonic friends.

I'm screaming in the darkness alone.
I'm screaming in the darkness alone.

INSATIABLE MANDIBLES

Damn!
What the Hell was that?
I swear I saw something staring at me from the back.
It was right behind me...
I swear, I saw it!
I am not losing my mind.
I swear, honest!
That thing that I saw was not human.
It was oddly shaped and so unusual.
Growling at me...
Then when I turn to it...
It's gone.
It's messing with me with its games and songs.
I do not want to play and sing along.
You have to believe me!
I am not wrong...

It reminds me of an ant with its insatiable mandibles.
Pinching and craving me...
I know what it's after.
It's after the one thing that it has always wanted.
It's after my soul and I am being taunted.
It could kill me at any moment.
With one quick swipe...
It would own me.
It likes to play and push away my sanity.
I must lose my mind before it devours me.
From the insatiable mandibles I am now screaming...

You have to believe me!

I am not wrong...
You have to believe me!
I do not want to play and sing along.
It's messing with me with its games and songs.
Growling at me...
Then when I turn to it...
It's gone.
It was oddly shaped and so unusual.
That thing I saw was not human.
I swear, honest!
I am not losing my mind.
I swear, I saw it!
It was right behind me...
I swear I saw something staring at me from the back.
What the Hell was that?
Damn!

You have to believe me!
The insatiable mandibles have sliced open my now broken back.
I'm being eaten alive and there is no back on track...
What did I do to deserve this?

This is a load of crap.

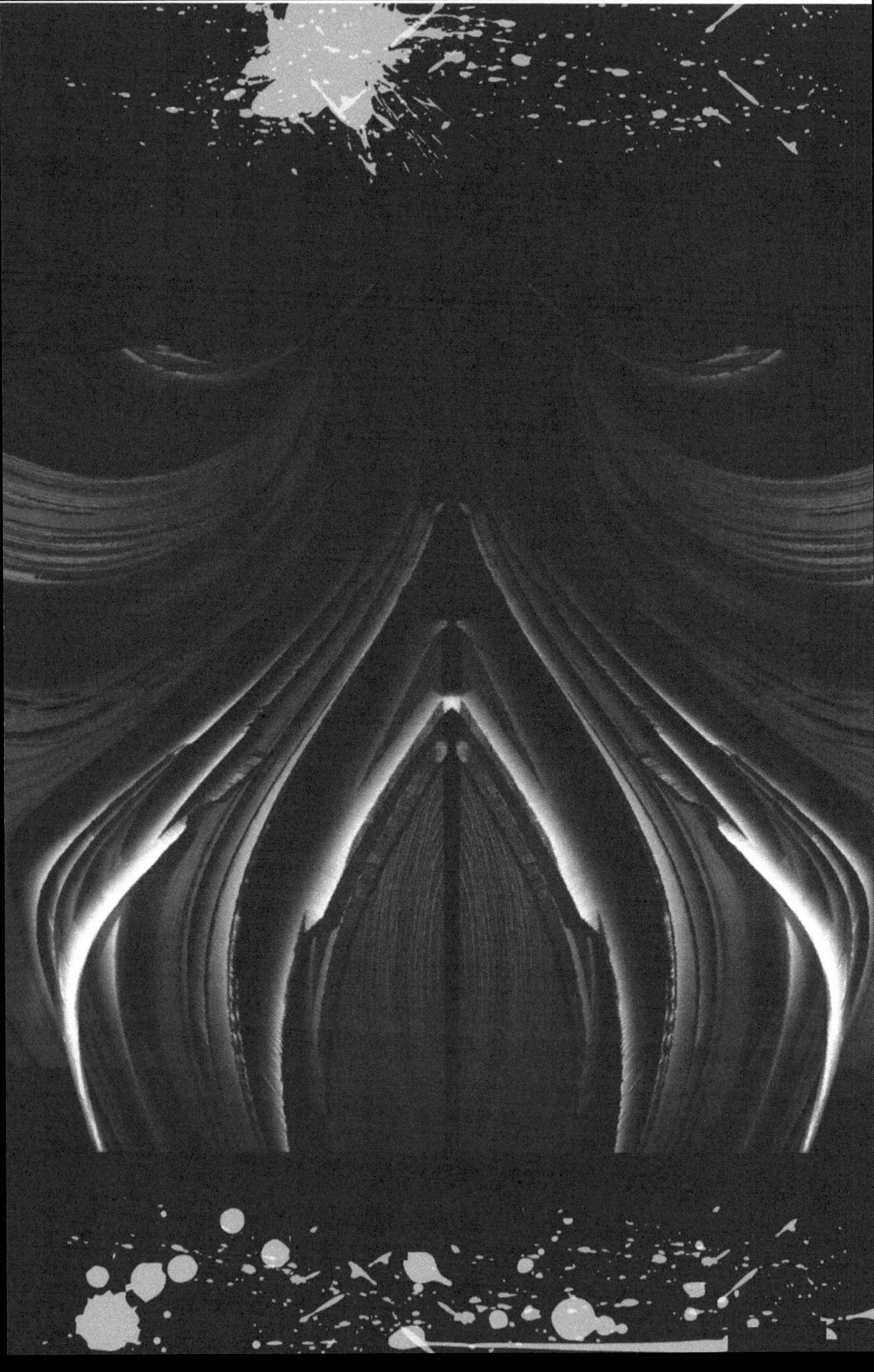

WALK AWAY

Never give your trust away to a stranger.
Never give yourself completely away.
Never give up even when you're in danger.
Listen to the words that I say.

When your guards come down.
That's when they'll get in.
They will tear your soul in two.
Trust nothing in whatever you do.

Demons are tricky.
They are so crafty.
They will do anything that you say.
They will take pleasure in you.

Demons are wicked.
When your depression controls you.
That's how they latch on.
That's how they feed.

Walk away.
All that creature will do is take...
Walk away.
Everything that it shows you is fake...
Walk away.

You've always had that choice to make...
WALK AWAY!

GO AWAY

I don't know what to say.
When you hit me.
When you hurt me...
Why do you treat me this way?

I don't know what to do...
How can I stop you?
I don't have a clue.
You've forced me to cut the ties.

I have dreamed of giving you forgiveness.
But I can't get past the pain...
I've spent hours trying to fix this.
Now I just need you to go away.

I don't know how to scream.
When you silence me.
When you make me.
Cover up the marks...

I don't know how to live.
Here it is so controlling.
It's unfolding...
Within my shattered heart.

I have dreamed of giving you forgiveness.
But I can't get past the pain...
I've spent hours trying to fix this.
Now I just need you to go away.

When I look at your face.
I see a monster.
I can't see you properly...
After what you've done.

When I look into your soul.
I see the fire.
I hear the screaming.
That's not what I've become.

I have dreamed of giving you forgiveness.
But I can't get past the pain...
I've spent hours trying to fix this.
Now I just need you to go away.

You've always been the manipulator...
And that's not what I've become.

Now I just need you to go away...

HEAD IN THE SAND

I'm lost in translation.
Some call me an abomination.
I can hear everybody laughing as I go mad.
I can see everybody staring when my smile turns sad.
I can hear everybody screaming as I bury my head in the sand.
I can't stand being crowded.
I can't stand being pushed.
I can't stand being grounded.
I can't stand being rushed.
I have a place in my head where I go to hide.
I have a place within darkness where I can feel alive.
A place where nobody can ever find me.
A place where I can scream in solitude...
Away from a world so brutal.

With my head in the sand, nothing can touch me.
Nothing can ground me.
Rush me.
Push me.
Crowd me.
I can scream so loudly!
Away from the voices that drown me.
In the perfection of my mess is where you can find me.
When I can't stand the noise of the people that pound me...
I bury my head in the sand and let the ocean waves become me.
Within their powerful presence, I become a part of the sea.
Then the power of life compels me.
I'm at my best when the hypocrites are not surrounding me.

I've become my own monster...
I've become free.

EGGSHELL

This thing has been following me my entire life.
Its skin is a pearly, ivory white.
It doesn't speak.
It has never muttered a word.
It makes me weak...
It makes my insides burn.
I don't know what it is to this day.
It just sits there staring at me making me lose my way.
Its purpose is obvious as it stays silent.
It makes my thoughts churn and become so violent.
It picks at my brain and smells of purple violets.
It serenades me into the light that is beautifully ultraviolet...

I think it was attached to me when I was very young.
When I looked at the cards it entered my lungs.
I was only a child, maybe seven years old.
I was killing animals and exposing their blood.
Is it an Angel of light?
Is it a Demon of darkness?
I can't figure it out within the chaos of this silence.
It doesn't speak so I'll never know what it means.
Is it here to help me?
Is it here to make me scream?
It's glowing presence rips me apart from the seams...

The eggshell colored demon is fucking with me.
This can't be an Angel if I keep feeling grief.
It is extracting my worst nightmares and using them against me.
I need to crack this eggshell if I want to continue to breathe.
I need to crack this monster before it becomes me.

ABOUT THE AUTHOR

Jeff Oliver was born in Baltimore, Maryland on April 6th, 1982. A poet by passion and father of eight beautiful children, his dedication to his family and his craft is second to none. Currently residing in Western New York State, he is a writer of intense emotions, having started composing his dark poetry at just 11 years old. His gift for transforming darkness to words shone brightly from a young age. Jeff Oliver's poetry has an ethereal quality. When others may have been destroyed from such a devastating darkness, he manages to weave lyrical justice into an otherwise unfair world. His published works include Venomous Words, Strange Sounds, Poetic Fiction: Journals of Silent Screams, Scattered Thoughts: Volumes I, II, and III, Drops Of Insanity, New World Monsters, Infinite Black: Tales from the Abyss, and Blood and Verse.

ABOUT THE ARTIST

Andrew first put a pencil to paper at 5 years old. Obsessed with the characters and creations he has seen in movies, by the age of 10 he knew that this was going to be a world that he could not escape. However classical music was a heavy influence on his work, as it would be on the record player as he would be drawing with the influences of composers such as Hans Zimmer, Danny Elfman and John Williams. To Andrew every piece of art whether it's on a paper or a screen is accompanied by a soundtrack. To him this only meant one thing, now he would have to start to play the music in the background including all the instruments such as guitar, bass, piano, keyboard, violin, cello ect in addition to creating his worlds on paper. Years down the road of being obsessed with art and music he began playing multiple grand venues such as the Gramercy theater, Irving Plaza etc while still pursuing art. Aside from playing shows he also composed various soundtracks and scores that can be heard in the movie Apex Rising produced and directed by James Terriaca. With the idea of the music conveying a scene, and the picture behind it, it began to take on a life of its own. With the visual effects influences of some of the creators over at Industrial Light and Magic, Amblin Entertainment and Universal Pictures, once Andrew saw the power of digital creation, he began working with Lightstorm Digital VFX and he knew that being the creator of all worlds in his imagination was inevitable. Being able to take someone away to a place, with what they hear and see is what drew Andrew to continue his passion of being able to manipulate one's mind with his perception of creation and innovation.